Caught Dead

&

Other Catastrophes

By
T. G. Browning
Illustrations by Mata

Special Thanks goes to a gracious band of people, who volunteered to help proof the manuscript. To be brutally honest, my proof reading sucks rocks, big time and everything I write is sprinkled with misspellings, extra punctuation and words, you name it. These people went over the manuscript for me and helped me find all of those errors. That doesn't mean there aren't any in the text—I have a disturbing propensity for leaving a trail of them just by looking at the written word. It's a gift, I'll grant, but hopefully, not inheritable. Thanks go to:

>Linda Earls, Cheryl Peck, Rob Bunyan, Tim Thrush, Roberta Sims, Betina Tasende, Rob Cowan, Nancy Anton, Taliesin MacAran and Elise Skidmore.

Elise deserves special thanks since 1: She was a buddy back in my old CompuServe days 2: Magnanimously compared notes on raising daughters and 3: Shares the same bloody birthday. She's been a dear friend for a very long, long time.

To Susan, Cassie, and Hilary, for all the laughs, and everything else as well.

Illustrations copyright 2004 by Mata. Published in the
United States of America by RDD Publications, 2170
Raynor St. SE, Salem, OR, 97302.

Cover illustration copyright 2004 by T. G. Browning, and
was based upon a photo taken at the south end of Main
Street in Toledo, Oregon, in 1958. Special thanks to Jodi
Weeber for locating the photo.

ISBN: 0-9753510-2-8
Published July, 2004.

First Edition.

0 9 8 7 6 5 4 3 2 1

RDD Website: http://www.revisedevilsdictionary.com
Mata's Website: http://www.matazone.co.uk

Foreword

These essays were written over a period of about ten or twelve years, barring only one, "Stumps From Space", which came from a talk I gave in an old time BBS chat room. A friend of mine had, unbeknownst to me, kept a log of the conversation and simply did a tiny bit of editing and released it into the BBS/Fido/Usenet universe without telling me.

And then promptly forgot about it.

Until about eight or ten years later when he happened to encounter a copy of the same file on a UFO BBS someplace in America's heartland. At that point, Robert snagged a copy and sent it to me with a note informing me that "Stumps" was the BBS's top download.

Thanks, Bob.

With that out and about, in sheer self-defense, I edited it and tried to turn it into some sort of format that could pass for coherent. You win some, you lose some.

All of the other essays were done after I attended the funeral of my Aunt Marg and learned for the first time that there's a place set aside in the Elliot State Forest of Oregon to park demised Brownings and Stivers. I wrote "Spring Planting" because, frankly, I was a bit puzzled by the whole matter and wanted to make a record for myself to look back on when I was either ninety and senile, or just going dotty on my own. It got me to thinking about some of the other incidents in my life and well, things just kept getting generated.

I've been told by some that these essays are unrealistic, not believable, too off-the-wall to be any good. I have never claimed anything for them other than they are, 1: By and large, true, 2: Not vicious, as some people's remembrance of things past often get, and 3: A reflection of how I view things when I have the equanimity to reflect at all. That's not always the case.

I save up the vicious stuff and use it either in **The Revised Devil's Dictionary** which I've been writing for about fifteen years, or put it in one of my Toledo stories. Generally the truly black humor ends up in the former and the merely dark brown in the latter.

I hope you enjoy them. I hope you get the point, most of the time, and do a bit of reflecting on your own about your life. What happens to a person isn't often under any sort of control whatsoever. About the only thing a person can control is how one views things, how one reacts and possibly, how much of a bribe one is willing to cough up to God, the Universe or Whatever. I've found over the years that James Thurber's attitude about things, as evidenced in **My Life and Hard Times**, to be a great way to make a point or to weather viciously ironic situations.

Whatever you do, read Thurber. He's the master and in many ways, quite a wise man. Short of that, find yourself a warm spot and do your own reflecting on the often bizarre and perplexing things that happen all on their own. Both are good therapy or would be, if you needed therapy. I find that the people who can look at things that way, no longer have any need for their head to be shrunk, even by an expert.

T. G. Browning
May 20, 2004.

Table of Contents

Caught Dead

This is the city: Toledo, Oregon. Population, 3132 people, unless it's a weekday, then the population hovers like a drunken hummingbird around 1400. From the top of Graham Hill to the depths of Rum Bottom, it's an archetypal Oregon Coast town not on US 101, which only means three things: It rains a lot, it's built on hills with its butt up against a river, and money is a sometime thing.

My first encounter with the town was at the age of seven. My parents in a fit of summer boredom decided we needed to see the Oregon Coast, so we rented a trailer and headed for Beverly Beach, north of Newport. We stopped in Toledo to get gas and ended up eating at Mel's Café. My Dad asked me what I thought of the town.

I told him I wouldn't be caught dead here.

God gets people with an attitude like that. He put me on a little list of things to do, waited two years and then flipped the sign that says "Begin Joke Now."

Thereupon, my folks went crazy, picked up and moved us to Connecticut, made my father tell the interview panel at his new job that he thought they were a bunch of pompous jerks, then plopped us down in a small summer lodge on Worthly Pond in Maine, with my Grandmother, two hundred dollars and no place to go.

Dad heard of a job and did an unheard of interview by telephone. He got the job, and then talked *the Man* into finding a job for Mom. After cursing softly under his breath, Dad then went outside and began going over the car with a fine tooth comb. Not only did he check the mechanical soundness of the vehicle, but he checked the seats for loose change, because that $200 had to last us across 3200 miles of road and two months of time before the next paycheck. Considering that I'd tapped out the back seat two days before for licorice whips (twelve pennies, a dime and a buffalo head nickel with a date of 191?), he came back inside with a remarkably cheery attitude. He cornered my mother and said, "Dickie, we better have a little talk." I never did find out what they talked about, but from this vantage point, age forty-three, I can imagine.

We took off across the country sometime in early August and my sister and I promptly got into traveling mode. This consisted of staring at each other suspiciously for any infringement of our sacred space and being told to pipe down by Dad when a border crossing went sour.

We rolled through the great plains in Canada, dropped down into the US again somewhere in Montana, had the car overheat a couple of times between Butte and Yakima, and then crossed back into Oregon at The Dalles. The next thing I knew we were camped out, way to hell and gone back in the Coast Range east of Coos Bay, the closest approximation of a town within twenty miles a one-lung place called Allegany. It had one store that doubled as a post office, restaurant, gas station and for all I know, a basement mortuary.

I found out thirty-three years later that Brownings get buried a hop, skip and a four-wheel drive away, up a cow path to a forest meadow that gets logged off every fifty years. But that's another story entirely.

We camped. Roughing it, my Dad called it and it was rougher than either my sister or I knew. Dad told me to have some fun fishing, handed me a pole, a couple of dozen worms, a peanut butter sandwich along with a can of pop and before I made it out of the tent, said that I didn't have to come back until I'd caught ten fish.

"How big?" I asked. Dad had always wanted to measure them, though at the age of nine, I really didn't see any point to it.

"If they can get the hook in their mouths, that's big enough," Dad said. That worked for me. Over the next two weeks I got to do a lot of fishing. I hunted crawdads and we ate them too. We ate a lot of what I suppose you'd call "really fresh food" that August, and by the time we moved on I was sick of swatting bugs, drinking water and eating dwarf sized trout. I figured if I ever ate another crawdad it would be at the point of a gun and that sucker had better be loaded.

I burned out early on out-houses, particularly at night, when you might run barefoot into slugs on the way to or from the necessity. My sister felt the same, but she was more stoic about it. I just plain bitched.

The week before Labor Day, Mom and Dad packed us up again and sprang for five used comic books at the Allegany Store (The Phantom, The Challengers, Two Archies, and a Classic Tales "The Man in the Iron Mask" missing the last two pages). We rolled north along US 101 which in 1962 was a broken backed mother of a highway where you drive through ghost towns waiting to be born. Reedsport. Yachats. Waldport. Seal Rock. I kid you not. The whole coast looked like a damp version of West Virginia, minus the coal and a working economy. Tourism was ten years in the future, people were hanging on by the skin of their teeth and scurvy looked endemic.

But I didn't see that, then. What I saw was: Toledo. Had a working pulp mill. Four working saw mills. Three grocery stores. A by-damn housing project with a house that we could get for $13,000 and no money down, your promise was good through the first paycheck.

It also had a junior high school that my Dad could run if said junior high didn't run him off like it had the last three principals. So what if it looked like something out of Poe's "Fall of the House of Usher," sitting on a knoll twelve feet lower than the pulp mill smoke stack due west of it?

All I cared about was that I would have a room of my own, a working bathroom and I didn't have to catch dinner. I loved the place. Still, I have to admit that when I saw the Main Street of Toledo and Mel's Café again, I remembered Dad's question and my sporting, carefree reply. I've been very careful in my replies ever since. The last time I was asked that same question was while I was having a cup of coffee in Boring, Oregon.

I said I could see living there. Only too well.

Coach

Like most US males, I ran into coaches here and there in my high school career, even in the small Oregon Coast town of Toledo. I admit that they form the backbone of rural high school life, the cartilage of socialization and the ruptured spleen of masculinity, as defined by America. But I've always wondered just how triple-A football coaches come to *be*. All I can figure is that there's a clandestine manufacturing plant hidden somewhere near Missoula for the west and one near Passaic for the east.

The ones you get in junior high school are nearly normal. They teach things on the side like math or history. I liked them. But the ones I encountered once I hit high school were a different plate of spaghetti entirely—and I chose the dish carefully. Italy gave the world spaghetti, Michelangelo and fascism.

Our new head football coach, Lloyd Kosaroff, was a trim, blue eyed, buzz cut, blond guy built like a brick wall with teeth. He had a few words to say before we started practice the first day, and we drew around him like a flock of penguins before an Antarctic researcher, rapt, intent, beaks hanging open slightly. He told us we had to work through the pain. We had to drive through it, crush it, obliterate it. Then, when we got through the pain, we would be, where?

Nobody answered. A couple of beaks closed, mine included, because I certainly wasn't going to tell a coach who wanted us to do something like that, where I thought we'd be. I wasn't that stupid. Billy Wienert, a good friend of mine and usually quick on the uptake took the bait and volunteered, out of embarrassment over the silence, I think. "Agony?" Myself, I would have said dead.

Brick walls, with or without teeth, generally don't have a good come back and Coach Kosaroff didn't, either. Small blue eyes focused on Billy, and Billy, actually much smarter than that last remark would indicate, got the hint and started running wind sprints without being told.

Coach Kosaroff went back to his spiel. He told us we'd be too tough to care where we were. Heads nodded. Then he had us spend the next hour and a half pummeling each other, and when we were sufficiently numbed, proceeded to demonstrate what he had meant by driving through the pain. I'd rather take a bus and leave the driving to someone else. Looking back at it now, I can't see how I made myself go through that, and the why of it escapes me entirely. Football wasn't that much fun to play.

Still and all, we had it better than the kids up in Taft did. Our coach was of Polish-Ukrainian extraction and his leanings toward fascism were mostly theoretical. The high school coach up in Taft was of pure Italian descent. His favorite movie was "Patton." He taught shop and had the Spanish Fascist motto, *Viva La Muerte*, on his wall. He believed in short hair, razor sharp reflexes, and feral but quick obedience. Val Tetrozinni, he was named. I heard that one history teacher called him Vlad, but I don't know that for certain.

The game between Toledo High and Taft Union High set new heights for sports frenzy that year. Our team was slightly smaller, a little faster, and at least three times smarter than the Taft team. I credit the increased intelligence to our not being required to hit dummies set up against low concrete retaining walls. The big thing Taft had on its side was that it was a home game, which meant the dual advantages of Taft officiating, and the Taft Union Memorial Football field, the only field west of the Ohio River designed with a reverse crown.

What does it do a lot on the Oregon Coast? If you guessed rain, you guessed correctly. How does a reverse crown work? Well, it's exactly like a regular crown except that the water doesn't drain *off of* so much as *pool in* the field. At low tide the middle of the field was four and three-quarters inches deep and the game was scheduled for about an hour before high tide that night.

Did I mention that the field was over a leaking septic tank? Must have slipped my mind. I'm certainly not a victim of repressed memory syndrome; I've been trying to repress memories of that game for over twenty years with little success. I was fortunate in one respect. I was a lineman and never got my hands on the ball. Consequently, I never had the need to develop gills like our quarterback did.

We survived the game and on one level, you could say we even won. On a deeper, much more personal level, many of us took months to recover. Both tackles and ends, one guard, and one halfback ended up with something that the team doctor diagnosed as the Taft Gunge, a persistent, red inflammation of the epidermis that crept with leprosotic speed from place to place on the skin, a kind of wandering skin infection that never got any bigger than your hand, but kept on the move, even at night. Billy Wienert named his Harvey.

I didn't get to play Taft the next year, because by that time, I'd been bounced off the football team for conduct unbecoming an athlete. I call it bounced, though Kosaroff told the team I'd wimped out and quit. The truth of the matter was that I saw no point in continuing when I'd been reliably informed that the next game I'd play in, would have God as the referee and would be held in purgatory. I saw no need to attend hell to get to purgatory.

Four years later, a long step out of high school, I heard that the Taft High School coach had been busted back to the junior high for belting a student on the rebound from where he threw said student up against a locker. The Toledo High coach had already quit teaching by this time and last I heard, he had taken up commercial fishing, a profession he was suited to. Fishermen have to work through pain all the time and I'm confident he's very happy now.

Down Time

Over the years, I think everybody encounters problems sleeping—whether it be a deficit or surfeit. Studies I've seen all agree that a large percent of the US population operates on less sleep than they need, which explains the allure of televised golf, bowling and Masterpiece Theater, I suppose.

Even so, there has to be a minimum quality of sleep before the full benefits accrue and therein lies my biggest problem and my wife's as well. Not to put too fine a point on it, my sleep patterns run toward a lot of thrashing around, yelling, cursing and more often than not, sudden leaps into the air that make my wife's rest a bit on the active side.

I come by it naturally enough. I've heard family stories about my father when he was a kid and how he sleepwalked, jogged, and occasionally ran flat out. If only half of the stories are accurate, it must have made interesting late evening entertainment for the rest of his family. This went on over a number of years and my various aunts and uncles have all mentioned—some more strenuously than others— running around the house in the middle of the night trying to catch *Frankie*, a strangely difficult task. Dad apparently could scamper with the best of them.

Dad explained to me when I asked him about it, that there was a set of semi-recurring dreams associated with each night walk. They all involved a redheaded man who chased Dad but never could catch him—he had even less luck than my aunts and uncles. All Dad could remember was having the vague idea that it wouldn't be a good thing for the redheaded man to catch up. Sometimes Dad managed to take the chase outside and I've often wondered what the neighbors thought about a pack of Brownings running around the yard and house at 2:00 a.m. I doubt that they found it reassuring. Dad's shenanigans disappeared after one memorable night when the chase had been particularly fruitless for everybody concerned. Dad distinctly remembers that he decided in his dream that enough was enough and took measures. Like a wounded Cape buffalo, he suddenly turned on the redheaded man and jumped him as he came around a corner in the kitchen. What Dad actually did was to take a flying leap at the refrigerator, which failed to dodge quickly enough, and managed to knock himself out cold. Dad's surprise move had left the rest of his family milling around outside and I guess it was ten or fifteen minutes before they gave up and went inside.

They found Dad resting uncomfortably in the corner made by the kitchen wall and the refrigerator and I'm not clear whether or not they shoved a pillow under his head or got him up to go to bed. While the pillow idea may sound a bit callous, I could understand the reasoning entirely. I wouldn't have wanted to get him upright and moving at 2:30 a.m.

That turned out to be the last encounter that my father had with the redheaded man. Since that time, Dad's sleep activities have been less strenuous and probably less exciting.

My own problems started back in junior high school, and the first time I heard about it was one morning when my sister, then in college but home for summer vacation, wanted to know where I had gone earlier that day—at about 3 a.m. I didn't have the foggiest idea of what she was talking about. She thereupon described what she'd seen—me clad in cut-offs, tee-shirt, thongs and a determined expression, jauntily leaving the house whistling something that sounded a lot like *Cocktails for Two*. During the rest of that summer, she noticed me doing the same thing three or four times more, though the songs varied.

A sleepwalker may
feel concussed
upon being woken

Other incidents occurred, of course. I suspect that my rather active dream life had something to do with my college roommate moving out in the middle of the term without an explanation or forwarding address. The couple of times I saw him later, he quickly made tracks in the other direction, but without providing any theme music as he did so. I never did have the gumption to corner him and find out.

Susan, though, has put in the most hair-raising time of all. I'm not sure what bothers her the most, but if I had to make a guess, I pick one of two possibilities: The jumping up unexpectedly in the middle of the night—often accompanied by loud crashing sounds as I collide with various pieces of furniture, much like a pinball that's just gotten trapped between the 100 and 500 point bumpers and can't get free, or the frenzied struggling with an assailant who isn't actually anywhere within a thousand miles of our bedroom in Salem, Oregon. In the latter case, she's been known to slug me when I get a bit too excited by the whole thing. That usually wakes me up. She doesn't pull any of her punches either, which I think is probably wise in the long run.

There has been some improvement in the last couple of years. I'm no longer shouting in my sleep, nor am I running wind sprints up and down the hallway anymore. I used to do that a lot during football season when I was in high school, running from my room, through the landing into my sister's room, and then returning. Unfortunately, I occasionally tripped over a coffee table in the middle of the landing, and more than once, I woke up crumpled against the wall with a big bruise just below the knee and a splitting headache.

In any event, the dreams I get these days seem to be a bit more sedentary. About the only recurring dream I get any more is the one involving a pair of Albanian dwarves, a pub and a couple of gallons of rather bitter ale, plus a sinister bartender who is never there when one of us wants a refill. I never actually finish that one dream and am kind of curious about how it might end. I suspect that somewhere along the line I'd end up confronting the barkeep and just hope it doesn't come down to taking on large fixed objects that happen to be in the vicinity. That may have worked for Dad, but Dad is a whole lot tougher than I am. I'm hoping I'll only end up going one-on-one with nothing larger than a blender.

Spring Planting

I have to admit that I've never given much thought to what I want done to my body after I croak. My mother figures she's failed me somehow by not instilling the right family values in me, but to be honest, I've always thought her views on the subject were just a little too deep in the outfield for my taste.

You see, Ma grew up in Maine during the thirties, where the ground froze sometime around the first of November each year and gravediggers took a train to Fort Lauderdale. Consequently, any member of the family that passed on between then and the spring thaw got to hang around for awhile as a kind of weird parlor knick-knack. Mom's earliest memories are of playing hide and seek between three caskets where Uncle Chet, Aunt Flora, and tiny cousin Wilber spent the three weeks that it took to scrape up three slots in a vault.

When she told me this I looked to see if she was joking and damn me if she wasn't serious. I looked to Dad to find out what he thought and he found an excuse to go out and rummage around in the garage. I never did get a comment out of him, nor could I get him to tell me his own views. I remained ignorant of them until this last spring when my Aunt Marg died.

Dad gave me a call and asked if I'd go with him to the funeral. I finally agreed after a bunch of long distance arm twisting, courtesy of my mother. I'm glad I did. It gave me a chance to see how the other half of my family got interred and it solidified my own feelings something wonderful. You might say it opened an entirely different vista.

Dad and I attended the funeral, and as we were leaving, Dad told me we had to head for Allegany next. I wanted to know why and my father pointed out that the whole point of coming was to bury my Aunt Marg. When I remained confused, Dad elaborated by remarking that the family graveyard was in Allegany.

I'd never heard that we had a family graveyard.

Now, Allegany's a nice enough town, if you like the rural life. It consisted entirely of a school and a general store, total population of under fifty, way back in the Coast Range on the Oregon Coast, up a fork of the Coos River. My family owned land up there, but nobody had ever mentioned a graveyard. I couldn't figure out where they'd stick one, since the land around did a useful approximation of vertical.

In Allegany, Dad pointed to a wagon track up an incline barely wide enough for a Toyota, and ten seconds later, we were deep in the woods.

We went up five or six switchbacks, saw one house, fourteen chickens and a nutria before we came to a fork in the road. I guess you'd call it a fork. The road went right and there was a locked gate directly in front. Dad got out and unlatched it, got back in and told me to go on.

I looked at the road and then at my Dad. Okay. I didn't have four wheel drive and Dad knew it. I put my pickup into first and we continued on. Another five minutes and we came to a place where two cars were parked—my cousin Steve and my Uncle Warren. I parked nearby and got out.

Other relatives started showing up, and we assembled in a small forest clearing that had cat tracks running this way and that over it. When I say cat, I do **not** mean *Felis domesticus*, or any relative. I mean cat as in John Deere, let's-go-out-and-push-several-tons-of-dirt-around cat. I didn't see any headstones, at least, any that I recognized immediately as such.

I asked my Uncle Warren where the graveyard was. Uncle Warren informed me that I was currently standing on the grave of my Great Aunt Ester. I looked down and all I saw was a stake painted orange. I thought at first he was joking, but he shook his head and observed that I might want to get off of my great aunt. I shuffled to one side and asked where all the gravestones were, if this was a cemetery?

My uncle pointed to a place over by four trees and sure enough, there were twenty or thirty gravestones "Why aren't they marking the graves?" I asked.

My cousin Steve butted in, explaining that the family who owned the surrounding land had been forced to move them so the cat could get through. The Plovers had thoughtfully replaced the markers with orange stakes and moved the gravestones to a safe spot. I could see what they'd done, but for the life of me, I didn't understand the why of it. Steve pointed to the northwest by way of explanation and remarked that the Plovers had a nice stand of Douglas Fir they wanted to log. I looked where Steve indicated and sure enough, about a hundred yards further on was a huge clear cut.

Uncle Warren, now the eldest of his generation, started divvying up jobs and I ended up mixing concrete in a wheelbarrow with water from an old ten gallon milk can. I looked around for a trowel and rod, but nobody had brought one.

A discussion ensued between the four remaining Browning brothers over where to put Aunt Marg. Uncle Dan and Uncle Warren wanted to put her by her late husband, but Uncle Keith pointed out that there wasn't room. They finally decided to put her on top of her husband and proceeded to dig. I watched with interest, wondering what they planned to do when they hit my late uncle's coffin, but my cousin Caroline shook her head and said, "Oh, they won't dig down that far."

I wasn't so sure. I mean, looking at the hole they were digging, it appeared to me like they were planning on putting Aunt Marg to earth in a locked and upright position. I was pretty relieved when my cousin Steve announced it was deep enough and wanted to know where the ashes were. I hadn't known she'd been cremated.

My Uncle Warren went back to his pickup, called me over and picked up something covered in a blanket. He pointed to the back of his truck as I came up and asked if I'd tote the gravestone. Another cousin and I grabbed it—a chunk of granite roughly a foot wide, eighteen inches long and six inches thick. Weighed a ton.

We deposited the marker next to the grave, which was now about sixteen inches deep and a twenty inches square. I looked around for the urn.

Uncle Warren unwrapped the blanket, pulled out a light green Tupperware container and put it into the hole. I nudged my cousin Caroline and asked her where Aunt Marg's ashes were. She whispered back that they were in the Tupperware. She didn't elaborate, but instead went back to a conversation with another cousin.

I went over by my Dad and stood while they covered the "urn" with some dirt and poured the concrete on top. My Uncle Keith tried to smooth the concrete but I could see he wasn't having any luck. Since we didn't have a proper trowel, I used the shovel to puddle the concrete and smooth it and then we set the gravestone.

That was pretty much it. The remaining four brothers, Uncle Warren, my Dad, Uncle Dan, and Uncle Keith, said a few words in loving memory; the cousins milled around trying to figure out who was buried where by the stakes, and I looked the gravestones over. I wasn't sure what I had expected, but the casualness of it all kind of threw me. Everybody agreed to meet at my Uncle Warren's the next day for breakfast and started fading into the hills.

Driving back to Coos Bay, Dad asked me what I thought.

I didn't answer immediately but finally managed that it wasn't what I'd expected. Dad glanced over at me, puzzled, and wanted to know just what had I expected? Something more formal, I finally ventured.

Dad thought about it and pointed out that there really wasn't much of a reason to be formal. After all, Aunt Marg wanted to be cremated and buried, approximately, where we had buried her. She was now resting with three generations of family. A big production would have been pointless.

I thought about that most of the way home the next day and I could see Dad's reasoning. I suppose I agree with the rest of my family, except on one point. I can't say I like Tupperware all that much.

This Here's the Thing

Most of the coaches I encountered during junior and senior high school were good guys that left few visible scars in their wake. There was of course, the fascist football coach who made some complications for me, and I've already written about him. There was another coach I ought to mention if for no other reason than the fact that I got a couple of jobs through him. His name was Dale Hargett, known generally as Daddy Dale, for reasons that will become apparent.

He was the high school swimming and diving coach, as well as track, and like a great number of coaches, taught both PE and Health. He believed in reason and civility and after getting your ears bashed with shouts and curses from Kosaroff, he was an enjoyable figure to encounter. His preferred weapon was, the *lecture*.

I got many of them over the years.

Daddy Dale was a calm sort of guy, a trim figure about five foot eight with short, curly brown hair going gray at the temples, and a weathered face with kind but rather small, sorrowful eyes whose color I can't seem to remember. I suppose the reason I can't bring their color to mind is because I really didn't focus on his eyes during the countless times Daddy Dale cornered me for a talk. I focused on his hands, which seemed to have a set routine of gestures that the coach started up and then forgot about.

Each lecture started out with a brief preamble which would lead directly to the same opening line. "This here's the thing," he'd say, and you then knew you had something between two and five minutes of free time staring you in the face. He'd make a "this wide" gesture, the two palms held parallel and vertical, moving up and down, and then his hands would go on their separate ways making some obscure, but no doubt meaningful, accompaniment to his words.

I was quite fond of Daddy Dale. And it wasn't just because his oldest kid was in my class and attractive as hell. Nor the fact that Kim was possibly the nicest, sweetest yet non-cloying girl one could find on the coast. Dale Hargett ran the city pool and did the hiring of all city pool employees, which meant that if you wanted a job that paid pretty good, didn't require heavy lifting, and more importantly, put you in a position to see almost all of the girls in the high school in swim suits, then you did business with Dale Hargett. That last reason actually worked for female hires too— just switch the spotlight from girls in swim suits to boys in trunks.

Daddy Dale had a kind of diversion program going, back before such things were called that. He and his assistant pool manager would keep an eye out for people who caused trouble in the pool with a blatant disregard for the rules. Once identified, such people were culled from the herd, so to speak, by first making them swimming instructors, and then later, after brainwashing, lifeguards. It was a sly trick that worked exceedingly well. He ended up with a bunch of lifeguards who knew how to break every rule in the book, and could be counted on to enforce the rules with all the gusto only a reformed criminal can muster.

One time, Bob Gilmont and I had a contest to see who could legally throw the most kids out during a summer afternoon. Bob lost on points but won on quality. There was this one kid named Brant who was universally disliked, especially by his friends, and Bob caught him splashing some second and third graders. I was back in the office but watched Bob give him a warning. The kid looked at Bob for a moment, and then turned to his buddy and kneed him in the groin. (There was a reason why everybody disliked this kid). Bob fished the victim from the pool and kind of poured the water out of him before he kicked Brant out for the rest of the month. I threw in the towel at that point.

Getting back to Daddy Dale, he presided on all of the swimming and diving team trips to various swimming meets which included some really long bus rides. The Coast League, as it was called for obscure reasons I always thought, included the towns of Reedsport, Newport, Toledo, Philomath, Albany, and Medford, the last three of which were all more than fifty miles from the ocean. My freshman year we had two trips to Medford and with the distance, we ended up having to spend the night at the Medford Hotel.

Picture it. The two teams, Newport and Toledo, always traveled together and almost comprised a single team in attitude. Throw in a healthy mix of about 60-40 boys to girls. In a hotel. At night. With chaperones who didn't have x-ray vision and couldn't be everyplace at once. The staff of the hotel asked the coaches of the Toledo and Newport teams to stay somewhere else after my freshman year. I think the staff was upset because they had to go up onto the roof at 12:30 a.m. to rescue six or seven swimmers who'd managed to get up there but couldn't find their way off the roof.

Don't let anyone kid you. We had an excellent time.

As a PE instructor, Daddy Dale had a long, unbroken record of managing to get every kid to *dress down*—don gym clothes—at least a couple of times before getting out of their sophomore year. That is, until he ran into a kid by the name of Bundt, Buddy Bundt, who managed to slip through every trap Daddy Dale could think up.

I have to admit Buddy was elite. He'd managed to go through junior high school PE with an equally clean record of never donning gym shorts and tee-shirt. All of this was accomplished even though no physical reason existed for him to be excused. He turned out to be a clever forger. He kept three or four excuse slips hidden upon his person, reportedly from a doctor or his mother or possibly his lawyer, all of whom swore he'd die should he be forced to run, jump, climb or sweat.

It was the stuff of an epic, that confrontation between Daddy Dale and Buddy Bundt, straight out of an opera by Richard Wagner. The showdown came sometime in February of my freshman year and it was painful to watch. I did anyway.

Daddy Dale confronted Buddy at the gym locker room door. He began as usual with "This here's the thing," and had even been going at it for 30 or 35 seconds before he noticed that Buddy, sporting a sanctimonious half-smile and holding out a yellow sheet of notebook paper, wasn't listening. I think it was the half-smile that did it.

Coach Hargett's hands started to shake slightly, but he recovered, took the slip and read it. He then crumpled it up and told Buddy to get into PE shorts, five minutes ago. Buddy handed him a second note. Daddy Dale snatched that one from his hands and, his face beet red, began to scream at Buddy words to the effect that Buddy would be out on the gym floor ready to run laps or by God, Buddy would find himself stuck in his sophomore year of school until Herbert Hoover rose from the dead.

And Buddy? He produced a third note, handed it to Mr. Hargett and slipped by him on the way to the parking lot. It must have been a lulu because a quick glance at the note clothes-lined Daddy Dale. He stood there for twenty seconds or so, and then his shoulders sagged, the picture of defeat. I don't think he ever even spoke to Buddy again.

I ought to mention that Buddy was voted *The Most Likely To Corner The Black Market* in his class. Perhaps that took some of the sting out of it for Daddy Dale—he could recognize genius when he encountered it. In any event, Mr. Hargett recovered from that one defeat and resumed his firm, vocal guidance of high school students as if nothing had ever happened. He was a damn good coach, bouncing back like that. I know I learned something from his example.

Never trust anybody named Buddy.

Garden Party

I suppose most people think their first few jobs are memorable, if for no other reason than the fact they actually get paid money and get a dose of taxable income reality at the same time. But I honestly can't believe that something so common to 20th and 21st Century US citizenry should be accorded such a title. No, to be truly memorable, you have a touch of the bizarre thrown in as well. Something that, if mentioned in a crowd of compatriots, could never elicit a chorus of "Been there, done that."

You know, like my summer of working as a skin diver at the Undersea Gardens. Do I hear any chorus out there? I thought not.

That was a weird summer, even though at the time it seemed fairly normal. The manager of the Gardens deserves (and has, I might add) a narrative to himself, so I'll merely confine myself this time out with noting that Jim had some peculiar habits and ideas. Even I could see that, back then, and I'm not exactly what you call easily ruffled. He did, however, run the place and put his stamp of approval upon all inhabitants and employees, which included a harbor seal named Herbie.

Herbie started work at the Gardens a week after I did, which ought to have meant I had seniority. It didn't. I was never sure where Jim managed to locate a baby harbor seal in need of employment, but had the impression that the Lincoln County Sheriff had turned him over to the Gardens, possibly in some sort of witness protection program. My first contact with the little blighter was after three days off with swimmer's ear and a raging cold, which made my introduction to my new swimming partner less of a trial than it should have been.

Herbie was, at that time, about three feet long, shaped like a fat, gray spotted slug with black eyes and a crummy attitude. Larry, my best diving buddy at the Gardens, would only say that I had to have Jim show me the ropes on feeding Herbie, and then vacated the diver's room to give a show. I nodded and regarded Herbie for a bit while he regarded me. After about ten seconds of this, he kind of chirped at me and crapped on the deck. As a sample of things to come, I suppose I should have been warned.

Jim didn't show up for a couple of hours, having duty at another tourist fleecing operation on the bay front, so I did my best to accommodate my new buddy. But aside from cleaning up his trail, Herbie didn't seem to be much of a problem at first. I thought about what I knew of the natal care of pinnipeds, which I admit wasn't much, and offered old Herb a couple of herring. He signaled his disinterest by urinating, which at the time seemed like it could mean something special.

It did of course, but I didn't tumble to his real meaning for several hours. Like I said, I'd been sick.

A little thought made me wonder if Herbie was thirsty, and immediately I knew I was going to need some instruction if I was indeed, going to have to take care of the little guy. I cast around for the day supervisor, Julie, and asked how to tell if a baby harbor seal was thirsty.

Julie regarded me calmly and with a certain amount of pity, I now recognize. She gently pointed out that as far as she knew, there were no drinking fountains of fresh water to be found off shore, so perhaps it really wasn't too big of a problem. Her logic was impeccable but still left me with no clue as to what I should do to make him comfortable. I said as much.

"Wait till Jim gets here. He'll show you everything you need to know," she replied before looking pointedly at the diver's room deck. She left at that point and went into conference with Penny, Jill, and some other guide I didn't know very well. There was a lot of rather anticipatory chuckling that went on after that, but I didn't know that at the time.

When Jim did show up, it was during one of the few ten or fifteen minute slots where I had managed to clean up the deck, and Herbie had run out of conversational topics. With a great deal of enthusiasm, Jim announced that it was feeding time and handed me a list of things to get from the refrigerator and bring over to the sink. Herbie looked a bit happier, so I bustled around and grabbed all of the ingredients I could find.

These included fresh herring—the ones I'd used hadn't been fresh—some wheat germ, cod liver oil, liquid vitamins, a can of condensed milk, plus a few additives I can't recall. Later on, we worked out a system whereby Jim would make up a gallon or two of the stuff and store it in the refrigerator for me to warm and administer later on. My attempts at making the stuff apparently did not meet with Herbie's approval at all. There's no guessing on my part about this, by the way. Old Herb turned out to be the only seal on the West Coast who could throw up ballistically on command, and...well, he did. On this one point, I was fully in agreement with Herbie. Lousy food has the same effect on me.

After warming it up to body heat and testing against his wrist, Jim took out a zeppelin pump, hose arrangement and loaded it up with about a pint of the mixture. The heavy, plastic tube on the delivery end was about twelve inches long and three-eighths of an inch thick.

"Watch me," Jim commanded, so I did.

He patted Herbie's head and when the pup opened up his mouth, shoved the tube down his throat. I would have thought the seal would have gone nuts at that point—I know I would have— but he seemed to be comfortable with it and began to look happy as Jim slowly shot the stuff into his stomach. It was kind of amazing. I wondered how in hell a mother harbor seal managed to work that same procedure at sea with no refrigerator or opposable thumbs.

Jim finished off another pint of the stuff and then advised me that Herbie wouldn't need to be fed again until right before closing. With that, he again disappeared, leaving me with the pup, and a huge mess to clean up. Herbie must have been happy about the arrangement because he promptly left a couple of notes on the floor and went to sleep.

I won't try to describe the before-bedtime snack I gave Herbie. Let's just say it involved several pungent comments on Herbie's part, a certain amount of blood flow on mine, and a whole lot of thrashing around. I did manage to get two pints into him which should have made me much happier than it did.

The rest of the summer, well, one could call it variations on a theme. I'd do my best to jolly the little guy into taking his meal without going three rounds, and occasionally he'd submit with a kind of vicious dignity that would have been notable if it hadn't been so damn painful.

I'm almost certain he planned each little skirmish in advance, and I'm fully convinced that once he discovered I had a weak spot, he concentrated on that. The weak spot happened to be a rather large wart on the back of my right hand, which Herbie managed to scratch, rip, nip and chew at random intervals throughout the day. Amazingly, the bloodstains came off the deck with very little effort, though I can't say the same about either my swimming suit or wetsuit.

Sly little tyke that he was, he always managed to time his attacks for those times when no witnesses were around—save once. I did luck out one time, and Sandy, one of the better guides, happened to be standing outside the dive room window looking in when Herbie nailed me once again. She told Jim about it, and Jim, of course, had a long talk with Herbie. When he returned he informed me that Herbie was sorry and it wouldn't happen again.

I figured Herbie was lying his flippers off and kept on guard.

Near the end of the summer, Herbie graduated to fresh fish alone and no longer required massive physical means to eat dinner. Coincidentally, that was just about the time Larry and I swam a western round-up on a school of lost anchovies with a seine net, and quadrupled the population of the Gardens in one back-breaking swoop.

Sometimes things work out. The whole summer I'd been taking flak for not being buddies with Herbie. I can't recall how often I was informed that he was "so cute," but it had to have been more than enough to brainwash anyone who didn't get bitten or scratched on a thrice daily schedule.

"He's so cute," they'd say, "how can you say such things?"

I'd mumble something and reflect privately that good looks and cute counted for a hell of a lot more than I'd been led to believe.

That changed as I said. That day the anchovy got dumped into the Gardens, Herbie lost it. I don't know if it was over-confidence or just plain over-indulgence, but he blew most of his support from the guides. He left holes in the school whenever he passed through, trailing tiny heads and even tinier fins.

What really upset the guides and the tourists was that by evening, Herbie was no longer eating the anchovy. He contented himself with jauntily dicing them up when he felt like it. His status as teen seal idol was ruined.

That's an overstatement, I'm afraid. Jim never did change his opinion. He was forced, however, to confine the little terrorist to one part of the Gardens by erecting a chain link fence to cut off Herbie's swooping attacks. After that, only those fish with suicidal impulses swam in the back part of the Gardens near the pipe from the sand filter. Last I knew, he was still there and had regained a certain modicum of popularity, now that he could no longer get into a feeding frenzy.

I guess that only goes to show that the melding of justice and nature takes a bit of arranging.

Dream House

I imagine most people have, at one time or another, fantasized about either building or buying the house of their dreams. All too often, one hears about friends or acquaintances who manage to be a bit too general in their fantasy and end up with a dream house out of Edgar Allan Poe or Stephen King. But, generally speaking, most people don't end up with such an extreme; they end up with something built by Frank Lloyd Wright over Love Canal or perhaps vice-versa—something in Malibu, but built by Gilligan and the Skipper, with no help from the Professor.

My wife and I have lived in the same 70's ranch style house for the last twenty-three plus years. We got the house through a bit of semi-legal chicanery that unfortunately, doesn't have a statute of limitations. I can't reveal the details but I had nothing to do with the planning or implementation. I just signed my name and looked confused which wasn't hard—I was. If you're a cop, keep that in mind.

The first thing Susan and I noticed was the odd address. Or should I say, addresses? That's right, our house has two different addresses. The realtor explained that the access to the house was supposed to be from the south side, but the contractor had dyslexia, misread the plans and put the garage doors on the north side. The realtor had no explanation of why the contractor had thereupon switched the rest of the house around so that the front door was the back door and the back porch with sliding glass door was the front door. The builder did manage to get the mailbox on the right side but that had been neither a lucky guess nor a sure sign of intellect. He put one on each.

The house was painted a kind of mushy-pea/vomit-green that took your breath away, if not your lunch. We managed to put up with it for the first six months before Susan took a close look at the paint and made the alarming discovery that a coat of less than 0.1 mils really couldn't be called a coat. They hadn't actually painted the place but rather, had dusted it from a distance and called it good.

We consulted our neighbor who owns a dozen or so rentals and who always seems to be cleaning paint brushes, about what we should do. Mel looked thoughtful and told us we might want to think about getting the place primed before we painted and to do so just as soon as the rains stopped. Primed?

Susan nodded and I followed suit. I didn't want to reveal that while I knew what a primer coat was, I didn't know why one would want to go and paint a house twice when one thick coat of paint might be managed. A little surreptitious research informed me that a primer was used to seal the wood, form a moisture barrier as it were, and give the house paint itself a solid, stable surface to bind to. The little handout I got from the hardware store even informed me that we could avoid blistering paint entirely if we primed the place properly.

I hadn't been worrying a whole lot about blistering paint, mainly because I figured paint blistered due to long exposure to a hot sun. There wasn't much of a chance of that, I reasoned, living in Salem, Oregon. Long spells of liquid sunshine maybe, or slime trails from banana slugs the size of a French roll—those were the dangers our house paint would have to face.

We primed it anyway.

We bought about ten gallons of latex primer and set to work sometime in June. The instructions were clear that one coat would not be enough to seal the wood so I counted on having to do the house twice before we'd get on to picking paint colors. We both went at it and along about half-way through the second coat of primer, I noticed something that puzzled me. I went back to the instructions.

Latex primer is supposed to have a satin/shiny surface once the wood is sealed and upon close inspection, the second coat of dried primer looked chalky instead. As an experiment, I slapped a third coat on and watched closely while it swiftly sank out of sight. You couldn't really say the paint dried. It just sort of got sucked into the wood while you watched. I showed Susan.

Susan's father had been a carpenter and she'd seen lots of houses get painted while she grew up, whereas my folks were strong believers in aluminum siding or moving. She got that look she gets when something terrible has happened and there's not one damn thing you can do but live with it—a kind of squintching of the eyebrows which generates two vertical lines between them, just above the nose. I've since learned just how serious that look is, but at that time, we'd only been married two and a half years. In retrospect, I demonstrated an IQ of about 50 by not getting panicky. Susan just went inside, got the checkbook and the car keys and then dragged me off to the hardware store. Again.

I was getting to know some of the people there well enough to be invited to Monday Night Football games, provided I brought a pizza with me.

About a hundred bucks poorer we came back with more primer, only this was an oil-based one that guaranteed one coat coverage. Susan muttered darkly that we'd better count on two coats.

"That'll be four coats of primer," I pointed out. "That's got to be overkill."

I love my wife and here's one of the reasons: She didn't immediately tell me to pipe down, or live with it, or any other of a dozen quick ways of saying words to the effect that I'm an idiot. She merely pointed out that one coat might work but what harm could it do to examine the surface once we'd finished that next coat. That made sense so I grabbed a can and a brush and went back to work.

The oil-based primer really did go on much better and looked like it might actually seal the siding. We worked like Dexedrined beavers all that Saturday and Sunday and finished up before dark, confident that we'd only have a bit more to do before we could retire this house project and do something fun, like have a beer and read a book.

We were optimistic, I think is the term. A more accurate term would have been delusional.

To cut to the chase, we put on another two coats. It took us a couple of days after work but we finally got it accomplished. In a moment of giddy overconfidence, I splashed on another coat on a three by three foot square of the west side of the house to see just how good a job we'd done.

The primer got sucked into the wood in under twenty seconds. The damn thing still wasn't sealed. It was better—we'd added about ten seconds to the process but that was about it.

We spent the rest of the summer priming the house.

It worked itself into a routine. I'd get home from work, grab a bucket and paint brush, move the ladder along the house and start painting. I'd paint till Susan got home. We'd have dinner. We'd both grab a bucket and get to work after the dishes were done and when dusk finally arrived, we'd clean up and go inside. I figure there were some parts of the house that got primed seventeen or eighteen times. It's difficult to say, really, because after a while, we'd just sort of start wherever we liked. I did notice that Susan almost always ended up doing a section that just happened to be in direct sunlight, her one beer of the evening carefully placed within reach. Like any native Oregon Coaster, I seemed to prefer shady spots, so perhaps between the two of us, we got most of the house done with roughly the same number of coats.

There was a kind of horrid fascination involved with painting about ten square feet of siding and then pausing to watch the primer get sucked down. As I recall, the longest it took was about forty-five seconds. It leveled off after that and stayed just about the same.

Ultimately, we were saved from total failure by a Dutch Boy paint sale at the local hardware store. The price was so bloody low for even their best paint, we couldn't resist. We bought all the paint we figured we'd need in the two colors we'd chosen and then grabbed four more just to be safe. We took a couple of days off work then and painted till our fingers could no longer hold a brush—and even then, I was tempted to throw bags of paint up against the side of the wall until it got dark.

Susan talked me out of it.

All in all, I suppose the entire enterprise can be labeled a valuable learning experience with the added plus that approximately twenty coats of primer and exterior paint added about two inches to the R-value of our insulation. I'm almost sure it added ten years of life to one section of siding under the bathroom window that had dry rot. But that and the second round of house painting is another story entirely.

Match Up

I was pretty good in most sports during junior high and high school, though I have to say, I did best in sports that involved water somewhere along the line. Not counting showering of course. This made a certain amount of sense since by preference, I spent from six to eight hours a day in the water during the summer.

I suppose my folks weren't terribly surprised either, now that I think about it. Some of my earliest memories are of the Prineville swimming pool and the three meter board. Anything that high had to be climbed and once up there, jumping really was the only reasonable course left open.

The fact that I couldn't swim at that time, only made the outcome of my experiment in gravitic acceleration more interesting, especially to my father who developed a noticeable twitch that summer when I was three. Dad never swam competitively, but I think several Olympic records in free style swimming lasted as long as they did only because he didn't. After the first time, the lifeguards put in a policy called the *Browning Exception*, which meant that they stayed on the lifeguard tower and let my father handle it.

My best sports, therefore, were swimming and diving. I was pretty good in football too, but that was largely because 90% of our games were played during rainstorms. Those games—and practices for that matter—where things were bone dry didn't go as well. I'm not claiming that the Toledo Junior or High school teams lost because of me, but I certainly contributed. A case in point was the first Varsity game I ever played, as a freshman, against our arch-rival Newport. We lost that one 81 to 0. I actually got five or six tackles on the guy who won All-State Fullback that year— Bruce Albourne. It wasn't as much a case of being really good at tackling as it was of my face mask being really good at snagging his cleats, which they did every time he ran over me. He probably would have had 1,000 yards rushing if it hadn't been for me.

I had the distinction during that game of sparing Toledo from the agony of a 82 to 0 loss by blocking an extra point attempt with my head. Our coach went over the rules line by line with the refs and they finally agreed that the *football* had to go through the uprights. A football *helmet* didn't count.

That may sound dreadful, but it was certainly better than my wrestling career, which left me with a huge aversion to spandex.

My junior year in high school I decided to go out for wrestling since I'd done fairly well at it in junior high and it was something to do during the winter that wasn't basketball. I thought basketball was pointless since you weren't allowed to tackle anybody who had the ball, and indeed, found yourself severely reprimanded should you get excited and forget. Wrestling was full contact on a semi-soft surface, and hell, it was only three rounds.

I looked at the different weight classes and figured there were like zip reasons to get down to 136, which that year had a senior by the name of Alan Blower controlling it. I figured I could make 141 since my normal weight was about 148, and briefly considered going for the 148 pound class—until I remembered that Eric Wade was in that weight class. Eric ran the 100 in 10 flat, bench pressed Volkswagens and had been known to hurt people just in the take-down. So, I ended up wrestling Pete Arnold, a senior who was quick, strong and just plain tough.

Match Up

Practices were...interesting. We always finished practice with a fifteen minute round robin sort of match meant to build up endurance and mental discipline. I can't say that I'd argue either point because they did, just not in the way the coach meant. Wrestling Pete certainly built up my endurance—fatigue definitely becomes of secondary importance when a body figures he's got one chance in ten of getting through the rest of the practice without broken bones. I know I learned to endure considerable pain in that process. I also know it took a lot of mental discipline to keep from screaming for help, which would have been ignored in any case.

I stuck it out for about 90% of the season, though I'm not sure I know why. It certainly didn't enhance my reputation with the female segment of the population in the slightest. Mat burns running from temple to jaw aren't attractive to most high school girls and that's probably a good thing, now that I think about it.

Since Pete normally beat the crap out of me during every practice, I was not on the varsity team—big surprise. I normally wrestled JV—Junior Varsity. I won about half my matches, which isn't too bad, now that I look back upon it. I probably would have finished out the season were it not for the fact that I got to wrestle one Varsity match.

I got the word during second period, that Pete was sick, and couldn't make weight, so the coach informed me that I'd be wrestling that evening. I suppose I should have been suspicious since Pete generally never had any problem making weight and had last been sick during the second grade. Along about noon I started hearing some ugly rumors that the real reason Pete had bowed out was that the match that evening would be against last year's All-State Wrestling Champion of the 136 weight class.

I started thinking about having a really big lunch, but the wrestling coach collared me on my way to the cafeteria, then shanghaied me to the locker room to check my weight. Since there had been no scheduled JV meet that evening, I hadn't been keeping my weight down and sure enough, I found myself 6 pounds over my 141 target weight. The coach hinted rather strongly that I had better start shedding the excess immediately or I'd miss out on my chance to uphold Toledo High School's honor at 8:00 p.m. when the meet started.

Wrestlers faced with the prospect of being overweight have developed some interesting methods to temporarily drop a couple of pounds in a short time. The human body carries quite a bit of weight in the form of impure water and on a hot day during the summer, a person can easily sweat off three or four pounds taking a brisk walk uphill carrying a small child. But, since wrestling season was smack dab in the middle of Oregon winter, and people generally went around waterlogged, a little ingenuity had to be employed.

A simple matter really. Stuff the wrestler into a Jacuzzi, crank the temperature to 105 and then keep him from escaping for at least five minutes. Two ten minutes sessions left me with the muscle tone of boiled lettuce, but I managed to get down to 144 pounds, just three short of my goal.

The coach, being pleased with my success, clapped me on the back, and handed me a roll of Cherry Life Savers as he pushed me out of the locker room to get to my next class. He told me I had it made.

It turns out that losing three or four pounds in a couple of hours is quite easy to do if one simply refuses to swallow. Of course, you have to do something with all that spit you normally generate, which is why the coach had also handed me a 12 oz. paper cup. I spent the rest of the day, even during my last three classes, either spitting or drooling into that paper cup.

Oddly enough, none of my teachers even commented on it, though my English teacher asked me to sit in the back while he read a selection from *The Red Badge of Courage* I think the Cherry Life Savers got to him.

To cut to the chase, when I did finally weigh in, I was exactly 140½ pounds. I immediately had a couple of large Cokes and started thinking of the match.

This being a real life story, you won't be surprised when I tell you that I didn't win my match. The kid from Siuslaw High School I went up against went on to take All-State that year in the 141 pound class, so even if I did get slaughtered, I'd been slaughtered by the best.

In point of fact, I actually surprised the guy. He knew the extent of his reputation, and was flabbergasted when the match started and I almost got the takedown. It irritated him.

I then proceeded to spend the next minute and eighteen seconds on my back flopping around like a trout who's swallowed the hook. I finally got pinned a minute and thirty-two seconds into the match. I'd like to say the guy had some respect for an opponent who had given it his best shot, but again, this is real life. As we walked off the mat, he told me the next time he wrestled me, he'd put me in traction for a month. Since District was two weeks away I figured maybe I'd just call it a season and go back to swimming AAU. I think this qualifies as one of those character building episodes that are often so painful. It was made even more painful when I discovered that my very own mother had given 4 to 1 odds that I wouldn't last a minute.

I'm just surprised she found anybody who'd cover the bet. I had the grim satisfaction of knowing she had to fork over twenty bucks to Billy Wienert, who normally had good sense. And I guess he did that time too.

I never did get a cut of the take, though.

Split Personality

Growing up on the Oregon Coast, I had at my disposal an enormous choice of summer jobs, of which seventy-three percent of them involved spending a fair amount of time sopping wet. What a set of choices: Teach swimming, teach diving, or life guarding. The summer after I graduated from high school, I vowed to get something that paid more and didn't require a swimsuit, but I ended up with a job as a skin diver at the Undersea Gardens in Newport.

My boss, Jim Wilkerson, impressed me with the concern he showed for his workers, telling me that as a diver, I'd be constantly exposed to disease and would therefore, not be required to do anything but dive. I'd have to watch my condition I was told, eat nutritious food and do my best not to come down with a cold or the flu. Jim wanted that clear.

That was all right by me. I didn't mind working hard, but I certainly wouldn't quit a job that didn't require lifting, running from point A to point B, or fawning on tourists from Great Neck, Long Island.

I learned how to give a show, what to mess around with and what not to (leave the female wolf eels alone, for example), and settled in to have a good summer doing something fun—skin diving. The first two days went very well.

Jim Wilkerson split his time between the Gardens and another tourist trap he managed called the Royal Pacific Wax Museum. I didn't see anything of him until my third day at work and when he came in, I was having a cup of coffee and a cigarette with one of the guides, Kelly. Kelly, about five-ten, slender, with blonde hair and a voice that required no amplification for a show, abruptly got up and went back into the gift shop, leaving me with the boss.

He had a peculiar expression on his face, an uneasy mixture of tension and manic good humor. He didn't say anything immediately but looked around, as if he'd lost something, going so far as to check the shower in the diver's ready room. When he came back out, he opened fire. He wanted to know how come I wasn't giving a show right then (the other diver, Larry Nelson was giving it), why I hadn't cleaned up the waiting room and what in blazes did I think I was doing here?

"Get off your lazy butt and give a show!" he said.

I could hear the show currently going on—we had a loud speaker right over the air tank rack. I went to the rail and looked; there was Larry holding up a skate's egg case with air bubbles streaming silver to the surface. Jim joined me at the railing and handed me my hood.

Okay. I certainly wasn't going to argue with the man—he signed my paychecks and I needed money for the fall term of college. I dutifully put it on, donned a tank, mask and fins and jumped in to give a show.

Actually, I hid under the lip of the Gardens, trying to figure out what the devil was going on. I stayed out of Larry's way, waved to the tourists once or twice and took to scraping the windows free of algae. When Larry finished and started to get out, I grabbed a fin and tugged; we had to have a talk.

Larry listened without a readable expression, shrugged and told me that our boss tended to be a trifle moody and thereupon got out and took a hot shower.

Moody took on a whole new spectrum of meanings for me, thereafter. Jim turned out to have a different personality every time you turned around and letting him sneak up behind you wasn't a good idea—some of the personalities had a vicious sense of humor.

Split Personality

There was the one time I came into work and found that somebody had cut a piece out of my wet suit. None of the other divers would admit to it and I went an entire week looking at everybody suspiciously, until I found Jim with a piece of wet suit material, talking to a representative from the front office—the Gardens was part of a chain of three or four on the Pacific Coast. Jim was briskly explaining how he wanted all of the suits the company was going to order to match the sample piece he had, whereupon he held up a chunk of wet suit for the rep, who nodded thoughtfully.

It was an odd conversation, particularly when you know that all of the wet suits the divers used—owned and provided by each diver by the way—came in what can only be called your basic black. They looked pretty much the same. The rep didn't appear to find anything odd about it, but listened and nodded, and nodded and endured while Jim explained his reasoning.

Another time, a huge school of anchovy wandered into Yaquina Bay and got trapped between a port dock and the Gardens. On that occasion, Jim appeared out of nowhere with a huge net bundled in his arms. Before I could so much as say, "hold the anchovies," Larry and I got to play western round up with a seine net, swimming the net around the milling fish and capturing about a third of them. You wouldn't think such tiny fish could weigh very much but we had a hell of a time getting them into the tank.

His most persistent personality seemed fairly normal except for a strange fixation with blue sharks. About twice a month over the summer, he'd track down some commercial fisherman and talk

him into hooking and bringing in a blue shark for the Gardens. It was a waste of good money and frankly gave me the willies. Swimming in the same tank with one of the seven known man eating shark species didn't exactly thrill me.

I finally figured out that he was hoping to achieve a world's record. You could say blue sharks have trouble adjusting to captivity. Not to put too fine a point on it, they don't. I heard from an Oregon State University researcher that the longest one of them had survived in an aquarium was three days. None of ours did very well either, though there was one that might have broken the record if an octopus hadn't dropped on its head and chewed his way through the eye to the brain, killing it. Jim nearly went ballistic when he found out and wanted me to hunt down the octopus and teach it a lesson. I pointed out that I still wasn't on a first name basis with any of the octopi and I might get the wrong one. He pondered that a moment before he stomped off to the Wax Museum.

Jim's attitude toward octopi took a turn for the worse shortly thereafter, when I managed to screw up and let one of the beasties bite me on the hand. One of the guides mentioned something about some species being venomous, but Jim shook his head and allowed that he hadn't ever heard that.

I wasn't so sure. After about an hour, my arm had gone numb and turned dead white up to the elbow. Jim finally said I could have an hour off if I wanted to skip lunch and I called the OSU Marine Science Center for advice.

The OSU people weren't very helpful, only mentioning that yes, some did have venom and that no, they didn't know if any of the local species did. Could I let them know how things turned out, click?

I took the rest of the day off and went to the Emergency Room, where they shot me up with several broad spectrum anti-venom samples they had lying around, plus a tetanus booster.

While I was gone, Jim started to plan how he was going to track down the octopus that had nailed me.

Shortly thereafter I had to quit work due to a ruptured eardrum. It was probably a coincidence, but Jim found a different job not long after that. I don't know that he was fired, but I do know that he had asked for reinforcements to stem an ongoing problem with disloyal aquarium specimens. He claimed the octopi were out to get him.

Feeding Frenzy

Growing up on the Oregon Coast offered a number of opportunities that you don't get in the Great American Heartland; jobs for teenagers seemed to pop out of nowhere. Many of the jobs had a few things in common: they didn't pay much, they tended to have weird hours, and they generally involve slaving for tourists who never did learn how to say the name of the state correctly. (It's Or - ee - gun, not Or - ee - gone).

Living in Toledo, a little town off the tourist routes, six miles inland from Newport, you'd think that the Newport kids had a better shot at the local jobs, but you'd be wrong. Most of the restaurants employed Toledo kids rather than Newport ones, for some odd reason I still don't understand to this day. The place I got my first "service industry job" was a case in point—Port Dock 3 Restaurant employed about twenty of my classmates when I was a junior in high school.

Elise Schneider owned and operated the place, and the work, while not easy, didn't pay much. Operating under some obscure exemption, the Dock paid twenty cents less than the going minimum wage. Elise was a nice looking, middle-aged plus lady, thin, medium height, blonde, with a somewhat dreamy expression that hovered just back of the eyes whenever you talked to her. She turned out to be the prime cause of the worst thing about working at Port Dock 3 Restaurant.

Paychecks.

Oh, we got paychecks every two weeks. They were all signed with a little itemized sheet that told us how much money Uncle Sam had taken, what we'd lost to breakage, and where FICA and Social Security took their bites. That wasn't the problem. The

problem was getting the suckers cashed. Now, I don't mean to imply that Elise was a dead-beat; she wasn't. She did, however, have all the memory capability of celery stored too long in a refrigerator. All the money the restaurant and bar took in sat in a safe for ten or twelve weeks waiting for Elise to remember to go to the bank. Consequently, the payroll checks had the disconcerting habit of not clearing. Calling them rubber was an understatement akin to saying you get drizzle on the Oregon Coast.

Nobody warned me about this little problem. I blithely went down to the National Security Bank in Toledo to cash my first check. The teller, a tall, gray haired old lady named Mildred, looked at it and pursed her lips as she shot a glance through me that had left holes. I looked around behind me but nobody was there.

She turned on her heel and marched to the day manager, leaned over, and whispered something. At that point he went from casually leaning on his left elbow to cattle-prodded rigidity in two seconds—about the length of time it takes to say the words Port Dock 3 Restaurant.

He glanced my way, gave me a polite mini-cam smile that should have graced a three dollar bill and sent her back my way. In a clipped voice, she muttered something about insufficient funds, handed the check back to me, and promptly closed up. She even shot a tiny little bolt on her side of the fence. Click.

Right. I went home and called a friend of mine who'd worked at the Dock for the entire winter and told him my problem. When Billy got done laughing, he offered to show me his collection of rubber checks—at last count, he had five that he still hadn't been able to cash.

Well, having a job teaches you a number of things, some of which are sure to stay with you right up to the day you draw your last breath. Cashing checks from Port Dock 3 Restaurant called for ingenuity, perseverance, and a touch of chicanery I've since not had to employ. But I still know how it's done and I guess that's all that matters.

I started casing places up and down the coast, looking for grocery stores, other *tourista* fleecing operations, anyplace where I might be able to get a check cashed. I quickly learned that all of the secondhand stores in Lincoln County had been stung by former fellow Dock workers. And I also learned never to cash one of these checks anyplace where you were more than fifteen feet from an exit.

The worst reception I ever got was at a fascinating place called the Harpoon Food Market, right on US 101, in the middle of downtown Newport. The place was an eclectic mix of gourmet foods, obscure (possibly lethal) wines, and pornography, circa 1970, which of course was pretty mild by today's standards. The owner always wore reading specs and an expression that could have been either a scowl or gas pains, you never were sure which. He seemed nice enough, wearily screaming at the teenage boys who kept pawing through the magazines. If you didn't do that, you generally got a lukewarm smile.

I cultivated him for three days before I made my move, buying a can of gourmet pickled herring, and two days later, a can of yak meatballs. The third time, I grabbed a box of Swedish wheat crackers that looked like they could be eaten without injury, and calmly asked him if I could cash a payroll check.

He smiled thinly and shrugged, ringing it up while I borrowed a pen from him and countersigned the check. He glanced at the amount and made change, and was just about to hand it to me when he clued in on the fact that the check had the name Port Dock 3 Restaurant in the upper left.

In the space of a heartbeat, the money zipped back into the register, the Swedish crackers were yanked from my hands and the tirade began. He sputtered. He yelled. He almost frothed at the mouth and informed me at a killing decibel level that not only would he not cash my check, he didn't want my business, not then, not ever! "Port Dock 3 Restaurant?!!" he kept shrieking at ever increasing levels as I left, my paycheck shoved back in my coat pocket, the Lincoln County functional equivalent of a leper.

Once every two or three months, Elise would remember to go to the bank and the service at the restaurant slowed to a crawl when the word got out. Waitresses, busboys, and dishwashers trooped surreptitiously after her. The whole town of Newport went on hold, as town people got out their own checks and quietly visited the bank. Tellers worked in shifts.

I didn't have the patience for that, so I came up with another method of getting my money, one that Elise wasn't fond of, but one that worked nevertheless. I had graduated from dishwasher, to busboy, to host by that time. Working the night shift I had to count up the till and zero everything out before giving it to Cora, the night bartender. About the third night I did this, I got an idea. The next night, I came prepared.

I simply signed my check over to the Port Dock 3 Restaurant and extracted my money from the till, carefully noting exactly what I had done on the tally sheet. When Cora looked at the sheet that night, she did a double-take and then glared at me. I figured I was about to get chopped up for chowder, but she merely took me back behind the bar and closed the door.

She wanted to know what I thought I was doing? I shrugged and did my best not to look scared, which I was—Cora had a nasty reputation as one of those top sergeant bartenders who took no guff off anyone. She continued to stare at me and I finally straightened up, looked her in the eye and said, "I'm cashing my paycheck here from now on."

Cora stared at me for ten seconds and then told me in a voice that could cut glass if properly directed, to keep my mouth shut about this. She put my tally sheet down by hers, gave me the merest ghost of a half-smile, and then stalked out to give some Corps of Engineers captain a double J&B on the rocks.

I dumped the money bag back beside the totals and sneaked a peek at her tally sheet. Just as I had thought. Cora had cashed her check earlier that evening.

Wood Working

I've never been sure how I emerged from my teenage years with so few visible scars. Ma would probably snort and say something about superior planning on the part of my parents—and there's an element of truth there—but I did manage to land upright a number of times on my own. I wasn't anywhere near as good at it as a friend of mine I've mentioned named Billy Wienert, but that particular comparison is highly unfair to make.

Billy had a Teflon exterior back before Teflon was invented. This was the sort of kid who could—and did—walk into people's homes, go straight to the refrigerator and rummage around for food without the benefit of permission. For some reason, nobody ever took offense. The worst reaction I can recall was when my father called out to Billy from the front room to keep his hands off the smoked salmon. Billy did as requested. I think he ate the last of the pot roast instead.

He tended to be brutally honest in his comments and again, nobody really seemed upset by his boorishness. I recall one time in our kitchen when Billy was checking out some leftover stew and talking to my mother. The subject of an elderly woman who attended the Episcopal Church came up and Billy remarked, "She's a nice old broad, but a bit of a thief." Ma didn't even blink.

A person can't learn how to do something like that. That's a God-given gift if ever there was one. I credit that same gift with saving both Billy and me from dire consequences a number of times, so often in fact, I more-or-less counted on it. Running around with Billy Wienert was never boring.

I have some Kodak moment memories that stick in my mind, all associated with Billy. Like the time we got to screwing around upstairs in his room and managed to drop a small box of books we were moving a couple of inches. It resulted in a level three thud, minor but noticeable. About four and a half minutes later we heard a slow tread coming up the stairs, followed by the door to his room opening in a vaguely ominous sweep. It hit the wall and quivered a couple of times, then we were presented with Mr. Wienert, a stocky man in his early fifties with dark hair, a ruddy complexion and the expression of those capable of telling something's a joke but who generally don't bother.

"You...woke...me...up," he said, pointing first to us and then to the ceiling as he spoke, as if we were witless children. Well, I guess we were, now that I think about it. Then he wagged his finger at the two of us, made eye contact and added, "Don't...*Ever*...do...that...*again*." He fixed us with a grim, tired expression for a moment and then slowly, like an old logging truck, turned around and went back down the stairs.

I don't recall that we ever *did* do that again. I'm still here, anyway, which certainly indicates we didn't.

Over the years, it always seemed that we ended up taking on the same jobs, working the same places, either at the same time or Billy first and me second after he'd broken trail. We both taught swimming. We were both lifeguards. We both worked at The Port Dock 3 Restaurant. I went on to tending bar, something Billy never did that I know of. He elected to continue washing dishes, partly because he was good at it and partly because he found lots to eat. He claimed he cut the Port Dock's garbage bill in half one summer.

When we both got driver's licenses, new vistas opened up and the potential for disaster got much bigger. Or would have, if Billy hadn't had his knack for mollifying any and all objections, complaints and disagreements the world threw his way. I seem to recall that I had misgivings about a number of our money making schemes but went along with Billy, partly due to greed I suppose, but mostly because I knew deep down in my guts that Billy would slip clear of any really major disaster. That had to be my thinking, as I look back on it now, otherwise I never would have gone out cutting and selling wood with him.

The Oregon Coast has lots of trees here and there, some of them on private property and a whole lot more on public lands owned by the Feds or the state or occasionally the county. Back in the late sixties, people commonly went out with a chain saw, a couple of splitting mauls, sledge hammers and far too much enthusiasm and found all the deadfalls and slash piles of wood they wanted. Billy got the idea that we could go out with his dad's pickup, a red 1966 Datsun that had a tiny five ft. by four ft. bed, fill it up with cut wood and sell it.

So, we did.

It was a lot of work. Far too much work for the amount of money we were going to get for it. I think it took us something like four hours to cut and split enough wood to fill up the bed. By that time I had decided that this was not going to be anything I ever planned to do again and started thinking about who the hell we were going to sell it to. The fact that it was July and winter was months away occurred to me and I began to fear we'd be driving this load of has-been trees around for quite some time.

I had no clue as to how much to charge, for that matter.

Billy did and even had a sucker lined up, although I strongly doubt that the word sucker ever crossed Billy's mind. I asked how much wood did we have and Billy looked at it for a moment and then guessed we'd have a half cord of wood if we put on a bit more. I looked at the pickup and shrugged. I wasn't confident that that particular Datsun had enough horsepower to get out of the woods with the wood we had. "Not a problem," Billy replied, without a trace of fear.

Well, we cut some more and split some more and stacked some more—actually, not very much more—and then loaded up the equipment and started back. The pickup managed to get us out

Caught Dead & Other Catastrophes

to the county road without blowing up on us and once we had regular blacktop to drive on, limped back into town.

Our pigeon was the father of a couple of kids ahead of us in school, Rex Edwards. His son dated the pool manager's Gestapo chief, Kim, and his daughter was on the varsity cheerleading squad and not only great looking and intelligent, but didn't sneer at underclassmen which is always appreciated. All of us, the Edwards, the Wienerts, and the Brownings went to the same church and Billy and I ended up trading on a common reservoir of faith to make our sale.

We pulled in headfirst, pulled back out, turned around, and then backed in. Before I knew it, Billy had me stacking the wood while he negotiated the settlement. It doesn't take too long to unload a Datsun pickup, no matter how bloody high you've stacked the wood. I had nearly done so when Bill came out with the money and helped me finish. I waved to Mr. and Mrs. Edwards as Billy pulled out of the driveway and we headed home. He dropped me off with my half of the dough and I decided a hot bath would be just the thing. I had no idea just how opportune my sudden desire for cleanliness would prove.

When I finally got out of the tub and dressed, I wandered into the kitchen to get something to eat and was startled to see both of my folks eyeing me critically. I got a sandwich and sat down and then they quizzed me on what I'd done that afternoon. I told 'em cutting and stacking wood.

"How many loads you guys get?" my Dad asked, leaning his elbow on the table and resting his cheek against his fist. He looked like a lawyer who's lost a case and has to be present for the sentencing.

"Just a load. Took us long enough," I answered before I finished my sandwich. It was about seven o'clock on a Sunday evening, and it was back to throwing kids out of the pool for me the next day.

My mother nearly injured herself trying to keep from guffawing and I have to admit I was a bit hurt. Hauling wood had been hard work.

Dad shook his head and advised me that from now on, I was out of the logging business, the wood cutting business, the wood hauling business and even the walking around in the woods business. He then proceeded to tell me that he'd had a couple of phone calls from Rex Edwards. The first had been to find out when the rest of the wood would be delivered, and then the second had been when he had found out from Billy Wienert that there was only going to be one load. He looked at me grimly and then asked, "Do you know how much wood a cord is?"

I wasn't up to speed yet and blithely answered that I didn't. Dad chuckled grimly and then told me that a cord of wood was sixteen ft. by four ft. by two ft., and I'd better keep that in mind if I ever wanted to do anything that might laughingly be called cutting wood again.

I hate to admit it, but the implications only dawned on me slowly. "I guess we shorted him, some," I finally managed.

We had, Dad allowed, not been very accurate in our estimate.

Dad and Rex had talked it over and when I saw Billy the next day I asked him how we were going to square things with Mr. and Mrs. Edwards. Billy shrugged and said something about doing some work for Mr. Edwards around their place. I never did find out what he had to do.

I always wondered if they had him clean out their refrigerator.

I Was Only Following Orders

Night's nice. I mean, when you think about it, it's a time to regroup, regenerate, and return to the simple things of the day. No traffic other than the inevitable kitchen snarl-up before dinner. No demand for quick thinking. No road rage. It's all shoved aside.

Generally that's the case. I imagine there are a few disembodied spirits in Waco, Texas that could clue you in on tense nights that just seem to go on forever—but don't, unfortunately. If you're not into spirit channeling, though, I can give you an up close glimpse of confrontation the short-side of mayhem.

It was dark in the city.

Forgive me, but I've always wanted to start a story that way. Of course it was dark—it was night and I was in my office checking my e-mail before heading to bed. Time was slipping toward 11:30 and the evening defined dreary, since my wife was out of town at a retreat in the rainy woods of the Cascade foothills. (I'm pleased to report that this time she didn't call to tell me she hated retreats). My youngest had gone to bed on time, as usual, and my eldest daughter, as usual, managed to mix Internet, three TV shows and a book into a quiet but chaotic, evening's entertainment. She had also finished up in the bathroom and gone to bed.

It's pertinent, by the way, that I'm hard of hearing and don't see too bloody good either. I had old contact lenses in, so my vision had an unearthly, filmy quality. My ears were in my desk drawer, happily whining to each other, which they're prone to do if you leave the batteries in them.

Suddenly, the door opens and Cass, my eldest, shoves her head in and yells "Papa, come quick!" I could tell she was yelling because I could hear her.

I grab a cigarette but don't light it because I'm trying to quit and follow her. I have to admit I'm not too concerned because Cass can go on better than any three people I know. This could be nothing more alarming than one of the cats being trapped in the refrigerator. Once inside Cass jerks back the kitchen curtain partway and points triumphantly, albeit while hugging the wall so as not to be seen outside. I follow her arm and see a bunch of lights in four colors and the three stages of blinking—on, off, and afterglow.

This is interesting, I think to myself and look at Cass for an explanation.

"Papa, it's the cops!"

I look back outside and mentally match up visible patterns with what might actually be out there in the drizzle, and come to the conclusion that, yes, by God, they could be police cars. More than one certainly, possibly even enough to form a flock or gaggle, or maybe a horde, depending on if they were in flak jackets, civvies, or in uniforms.

I tell Cass to stay inside—she is, after all, in her pajamas—and step out on to the front stoop. Over the light patter-pit of massive rain drops, I can hear what might be sirens somewhere in the distance.

I peer around and make out a few figures behind the headlights and take a couple of steps, only to have a vicious voice command me, "Get back in the mouse." I ponder that for a moment, make a shrewd guess that the voice probably said house rather than mouse and slowly back up, hands held away from my sides. I don't know there are guns pointed at me, but it looks like a reasonable guess under the circumstances.

Once back inside, Cass peppers me with questions, none of which I can answer this early in the narrative. I'm afraid I'm a tad abrupt when I tell her to get dressed, pronto, and head for Hilary's room.

Hilary's room faces the other side of the house and she's dead to the world when I flip on the light and give her a gentle shake. She bats at my hand a couple of times and then opens an eye and glares at me.

"Get up," I say, shaking her shoulder with a bit more authority. "Get up, get dressed, and get to the kitchen. Now."

Knowing her, I wait to make sure that she actually completes step one and then go back out to the kitchen.

When you reach the middle of middle age, most people acquire the ridiculous notion that they have a firm idea of what should be done in all crises. It's patently absurd but I think most people harbor that notion, deep down. I know I did.

The fact remains, however, that a couple of hours of hard thinking still wouldn't give me a solid idea of the best course of action to take when there are a half-dozen or so surly cops stomping around outside the front door. The NRA be damned; pulling out a gun is not a good idea. I don't think turning on the TV and watching a late movie is an option, either.

After a couple of minutes, I decide that one of the cops might be a little less rushed and can answer a couple of innocent questions, so I elect to give it another go. I step out, light my cigarette in the hope that the police would reason that anybody stupid enough to smoke in the middle of an emergency is a mental defective and therefore harmless—only to have another voice snarl at me before I get two soggy steps.

"You! Stop right there." I stop right there.

"Turn around." I turn around.

"Walk backwards toward me!" Tilt...Gotta think about this.

Ever since I had an unfortunate episode in fifth grade gym class involving Newton's laws, running backwards and waking up on cold cement, I've never really cottoned to doing anything

Turn around and walk backwards...

Now hop...

Pat your head and rub your tummy...

Hop on one leg...

backward. Not to put too fine a point on it, you want me to move backward, you give me a mirror. I'm generally pretty firm about that.

This looks like a wizard time to make an exception.

I turn around carefully, arms away from my side—I had a hunch guns were still a good bet—and step slowly backwards. Long about step number six, I hear "Get Jack inside! Now!"

I look around for somebody named Jack, strike out completely and make a guess that the cop is yelling at me—my second shrewd guess of the evening. I figure this better wind up pretty damn quick because I've used my quota of shrewd for the week. I make slow tracks back into the kitchen.

During this, our dog Nikki, a Samoyed, has kept a low profile under the living room coffee table. When I come back in the second time, he trots over to the kitchen door, sits down and regards all of the activity for a couple of seconds. Thereupon he looks at Cass, looks back outside and comes to some eminently sensible dog decision. He parks himself in the utility room and stares pointedly at his leash. Cassie observes that the dog's sharper than he looks.

Myself, I'm not partial to the idea of either a leash or handcuffs. I'm still dredging my brain for what I should be doing. I ponder for a moment longer and then figure what the hell, let's try 911. It's an emergency, right?

I dial it. Cass notices what I'm dialing and looks at me like I've lost my mind.

A clear, crisp voice wants to know what my emergency is and I'm kind of at a loss for a moment. Well, I tell the dispatcher, I'm not sure. You see I've got a bunch of excited cops outside and I can't figure out what they want me to do. I look back outside and watch some flashlights play over our hedge, my pickup and a pile of willow tree chunks from a storm three years ago that I suppose I ought to get shed of.

I get a kind of pregnant, hissing pause on the phone that might signal consternation but could mean they're tracing the call. I wonder why the cops can't afford Caller ID as Cass grabs my arm and tugs, none too gently. "Just a minute," I manage and look toward the door. Standing outside is a burly cop clutching a shoulder mike and looking grim, excited, and enthusiastic all at the same time. This doesn't make me feel any better somehow, but I tell the cop on the phone that I have a cop at the door, what do I do?

I get phone hiss again for a full five seconds and then in a disgusted voice, I get the observation that I might consider opening the door to see what he wants. Then 911 hangs up on me.

I have Hilary grab Nikki, already leashed, open the sliding glass door cautiously and peer at our visitor.

He informs me in a voice that, thank God, is loud, clear and would do well on any stage in the country, that they've just busted some guy after a car chase and are still chasing the driver of the car. He takes one look at Nikki and advises us to keep our dog in, because they have police dogs running around as well. Further, I'm informed, he's sorry about yelling at me but in point of fact, they were yelling at the passenger in the suspect car who was trying to sneak off—didn't mean me at all.

I admit I'm a bit relieved to hear I'm not going to be arrested, handcuffed or shot and start to try to get the details of the situation when the radio crackles and our cop cuts me off. It appears that Benny the police dog has managed to lay teeth on the escaped driver on the other side of our house, and currently has the driver down on the sidewalk while he takes a snack break. Later, according to the neighbors, I understand that Benny is the largest German Shepherd they've ever seen and that the suspect spent the better part of twenty minutes howling something about bites, bones and blood. I'll have to take their word about that.

I Was Only Following Orders

The cop comes back after a moment and tells me the fun's over and I can go back to bed, don't let the dog out, ignore the lights, have a nice evening, goodbye and hotfoots it around our hedge, down the alley and up Clark Creek headed for the far side of the house, where two more cop cars have showed up. All in all, it turns out we had five squad cars in our alley, one escape vehicle that didn't, two more cop cars one block north of us running up and down the street, one on Electric Street by the creek and a total of four on Hoyt Street, which is where Benny took the driver into custody.

As I watch the cops still milling around, Cassie again tugs on my arm.

"Why call 911, Papa?" she asks. "We had enough cops running around as it was. Why call for more?"

I shrug helplessly. "I dunno. Seemed like a good idea at the time." She shakes her head and bustles Hilary back to bed, not buying my lame answer. No way I am going to tell her that I've never had the chance to call 911 and couldn't let it slip by. My reputation is flaky enough as it is.

The Luggage

I want one thing perfectly clear, right at the start. I am not superstitious. I don't believe in alien conspiracies, channeling, crystal healing, ESP or pyramid power. Nor do I consider the Theory of Atlantis, the prophecies of Edgar Cayce, television infomercials, campaigning politicians or Ouija boards to be within spitting distance of the truth.

Now that that's established, I have to say that I'm facing a second trip to Europe and after the first one to England, I decided to take precautions—I'm going to avoid a replay of the peculiar problems of the last trip. To further that end, when Susan, my wife, suggested that we might want to check out a luggage sale at a local store, I leapt at the chance.

You see, after years of traveling with my folks, who believe that anything not taken will surely be missed, the idea of getting something for my stuff that weighed less than a ton, couldn't hold the front four of a football team, and didn't set off alarms at airports, was more than welcome. You bet, I leapt.

This isn't to say that my folks might have changed their ways. Don't be ludicrous. Even as I write, my folks are abroad, in Italy, with only slightly less than the supplies the Allies used for the landing at Anzio. Considering Ma had a 60 pound weight limit, it's nothing short of miraculous just what my mother crammed into one of those stand-alone, wheeled, pull-cart pieces of luggage. She may have discovered how to warp space and put more than one object in one spot. That would explain how she manages to carry a sewing kit, a medical kit, water, a change of clothes, a camera and film, passport, a compass, a pocket knife, a world atlas, and a Clark bar in a fanny pack.

The Luggage

I've always wondered what would happen to a thief who managed to steal that pack. Opening it without taking the proper precautions isn't something I would try. I imagine the effect would be similar to the detonation of a letter bomb, but that's just speculation on my part.

Just prior to our England trip, my folks bought both Susan and I one of the pieces of luggage that sits back on a third, small nubbin and looks like a square R2-D2. Huge is a feeble description. I had my youngest daughter, Hilary, see if she could get into it and she could. Easily.

I suppose we could have saved on the price of a ticket if we'd put air holes in M&DL (Mom & Dad Luggage) but I didn't cotton to the hassles we might encounter at customs. So, when the time came, Susan dutifully packed it and we set off.

I didn't run into any real problems until we boarded the bus to leave Heathrow. M&DL was a half inch too thick to go in 90% of the compartments and it was only by dint of Herculean effort on my part, plus a bribe to the driver for help, that we managed to get it stowed away.

Once in Bath, we had planned on taking one of the taxis that Bath brochures maintain are always available, only to discover that the luggage my folks had picked out managed to be impossible to cram into most all of the cabs. A wait of about a half-hour netted us one of the old cabs you see in all those black & white war films with dashing RAF pilots. Or rather, it would have if some jerk from Turkey and his family of 9 hadn't blitzed us and piled in before we could even begin a counter-attack.

Susan said I was on vacation to have *a good time*, so I should just let it pass. That was a very wise suggestion, considering the problem I encountered once we got to our hotel. Stairs. Three flights of them.

The hotel manager proved to be a perfect, considerate host. He even showed us to our rooms on the fourth floor, which was nice of him, though I did note that he made a point of warning me to be careful of the walls since they'd just been painted and the stairway was narrow. "Very narrow," he said. "Don't touch the brass railing; it's brand new."

I can recognize a veiled threat when I hear it, even if it's in light, cheery tones; I did my best not to let M&DL, my computer, and two carry-on bags bump into anything, and pondered things while I rested on each landing. One of the conclusions I came to on the first landing was that landings were a marvelous invention and should be encouraged in all modern buildings.

I also came to the realization that Newton had only been partly correct with his theory of gravity. The way it's supposed to work, the further apart objects are, the less mutual attraction they experience. On landing three, it occurred to me that, this high up, each piece of luggage should be lighter—heck, we had climbed nearly a mile of steps. The damn thing should have dropped a couple of pounds at that distance. But if anything, the damn thing had gained twenty or thirty pounds. I looked at it speculatively and I swear the damn thing had a smirk to it.

Once in the room, I stowed M&DL with the rest of the luggage and put it out of mind. We only had three days in Bath and we needed to map out where and what we planned on doing. That took the rest of the evening.

Now here's the weird thing. It seemed like every time we came back from an outing over the next three days, one particular, looming piece of luggage had moved. The first time, it was at the foot of our bed and some time later it was parked right next to the bed on my side. I didn't start getting really spooked until our last day in Bath when I fell over it coming out of the bathroom after my shower. M&DL had been leaning against the door.

I kept an eye on it after that. I never caught it rolling around by itself—but there were too many times when I knew Susan and both of the kids couldn't have moved it. I began to worry about trying to get that damn thing out of the hotel and down to a cab and the more I worried, the more often I discovered M&DL leering at me.

Ultimately, I knew it was going to be a case of *it* or *me*.

That night, I took steps. I assembled my reasons, discarded the ones that would prove me insane, and presented an idea to Susan. I had noticed that there was a tourist shop about a block from the hotel and told Susan that we might be able to find a good buy.

My wife doesn't shop all that much, being of a frugal nature, but the idea of getting something at 60% off appealed to her so she accompanied me to the store. Once there, I parked her in umbrellas and top coats, grabbed a piece of luggage that was only twenty inches tall and looked incapable of carrying complete wardrobes. It also showed no sign of a smirk nor any hint of sentience; I bought it before Susan could come up with an objection.

She was puzzled, but I put off an explanation until we got back to the hotel.

Once there she wanted to know what I thought I was doing.

I replied that I was merely trying to protect myself. I reminded her that the stairs were narrow and that the hotel manager had already nicked one of our neighbors for a scuff mark on the wall. Further, there was the problem of getting a cab that could carry everything.

Susan pointed out in that reasonable tone she takes when I'm completely around the bend over something, that we were close enough to walk to the bus station. That left me nothing to tell her but the truth which I did—very, very carefully.

I explained how the piece of luggage that Mom and Dad had bought us was out to get me. How it was a hell of a lot smarter than it looked, and would probably succeed before the trip was over, and how would she like to be a widow? She certainly listened closely, I'll give her that.

"So what are we going to do with it? Ship it home?" she asked.

I replied that it cost too much, and besides, we didn't know exactly where to drop a package off, anyway. She nodded. She'd thought of that.

She waited for an answer.

"I say let's ditch it."

She regarded me for a moment before pointing out that it was an expensive present from my folks. How would we explain the loss?

I replied that we could say it had been stolen by a huge deaf-mute wearing a turban. He'd have to be huge I pointed out, to manage to move it.

Susan is shrewd, beautiful, and utterly pragmatic about unpleasant facts. My answers had convinced her that we had to get rid of M&DL, if for no other reason than to preserve my fragile hold on reality. "So how do we get rid of it?"

I had mapped out a couple of plans in my mind and related my best scenario. The two of us would sneak it outside after dark and leave it in the park two blocks over. I stoutly maintained that it wasn't littering because it was obviously valuable, if not actually cursed. Somebody would be happy to take possession of it. Maybe make a few bucks selling it. We'd be shed of the thing before you could say slipped leash, let alone slipped disc. I could tell she didn't think much of the idea but she was tired, didn't like M&DL much herself, and knew from over twenty years of marriage to me, that I'd have at least three more ideas ready if she rejected this one. She agreed.

"If we get caught, I don't know you," she said. That seemed fair enough to me.

Look, they don't understand crop circles, let's try moving their luggage instead.

That's what we did. We had a bad moment getting it past the hotel owner who always seemed to be lurking around, but we did, and briskly trundled M&DL over to the park. By sheer good fortune, we found where there was a central collection point for park stuff, and I managed to stuff M&DL between a wheel barrow and what looked like a portable volleyball pole. I also put five or six decorator bricks on top, hoping to slow it down some.

On the way back, Susan noticed I still seemed nervous and asked me why. The deed was done.

I didn't answer immediately; my stomach was tight and I could hear the strains of the Twilight Zone theme floating on the wind. Susan nudged me, forcefully, in the ribs and I gave up.

I finally told her of my fear—that M&DL would be back in our hotel room waiting for us when we got back. "It was too easy," I said. "It was toying with us."

Susan laughed and told me I was silly. To this day, she maintains that.

All I can say is that I noticed that she kept glancing over her shoulder as we walked back.

Give It A Rest

I've become accustomed to getting phone calls from people at all hours of the day or night. That started a number of years ago when I was a freelance programmer and began to get telephone queries and requests for program support from places like Innsbruck, Manchester and Munich. There's nothing quite like getting a phone call at 2:00 a.m. and being asked, in a thick German accent, why my program wouldn't run on a Macintosh. I suppose it was that ennui that allowed me to take my mother's purchase of a computer without even blinking.

My mother, at the time of this writing, is 79 years old and gets around better than most people just crossing the border of 60. To be more accurate, the lady is a pistol. I can't think of any other woman or man her age who's had the guts to jump into the MS-DOS world of computers for no other reason than interest. She did have the advantage of a son who worked as a programmer, but nine programmers out of ten will tell you all that means is that the explanations are not only confusing, but technically correct. I figure the long distance calls paid for at least one communications satellite.

And you know? Ma ends up going places in computer programs that I have never been able to find, let alone be familiar with. I don't know how she does it, but every so often she ends up in some goofy subroutine that a bored programmer slipped into the shipped code.

If you're not much into computers, I had better explain that.

You see, most of the really big programs, ones that do things like word processing or heavy-duty number crunching like Excel or the old Lotus 1-2-3, are written and maintained by teams of programmers. They spend countless hours writing and debugging code and while it may sound interesting, quite a lot of it is boring. So, to keep sane, they write little routines that do something odd—send a message to the screen, change the look of the program—something like that. Over the years, it's become standard practice for teams to leave some of this code in the shipping product, but hidden. Normally, the user never encounters it. Such little jokes or oddities are called Easter Eggs and there are some people who specialize in tracking them down. It's become kind of a bent scavenger hunt, particularly in games like *Gabriel Knight* or *Indiana Jones*.

My mother finds them.

A lot.

I remember the first time, back before Ma switched to Windows 95. She called, spooked as hell. She had the feeling that the printer was out to get her—not really such a daft idea if you've ever done much with printers—and wanted to know what she should do.

"Well, what happens?" I asked.

Ma sighed and related a dismal tale of betrayal and sudden death, all involving her latest letter to cousin Molly back in Maine. Seems she had the printer all ready to go and from within Word, told the program to print by going right straight through the menu options, just like always, and then...nothing.

The dialog box went away and Mom thought okay, and went to pour some coffee. When she got back, the printer hadn't put anything on paper.

It hadn't even advanced the paper.

It didn't even deign to blink a light to complain about being jammed or upset or mildly peeved.

"It just sat there and looked at me."

I muttered my usual observation about printers—they're just smart enough to get confused—and walked her through it over the phone.

No problems. Printer started printing. Ma grumbled she'd done exactly the same thing and gotten nowhere. Not much I could say to that. I've had my own skirmishes with printers to keep me amused, so I hung up and went about my business.

Now here's where Ma's secret talent comes into play. No bloody printer was going to get away with that, so Mom set things up again and had Word print out the same letter a second time.

The printer turned itself off.

I wish I'd been there for what happened next. With grit and determination and a lack of philosophic balance, Ma did it again. The printer just sat there this time. To cut to the chase, she spent the next hour and a half trying to get that bloody printer to print and got zip for her efforts. And then she ran into the *Easter Egg.*

She turned off the printer, exited the program, restarted the program and the printer and opened her letter. She took the menu option to print, just like always, and sent the command to the printer.

Success! The printer did something!

It ejected four sheets of paper and turned itself off while a message dialog box appeared on the monitor that said, and this is a direct quote (Ma wrote it down): "Give It a Rest, Can't Ya?"

Ma sat and stared at the screen. She checked the clock, saw it was already nearly midnight and very carefully closed up shop. Shut everything down and then left the room. Had I not known about Easter Eggs, I would have done that and topped if off by locking the door. Calling it spooky was putting it mildly.

After this happened a couple of times more, she finally called and in an awed voice, she related the incident. I could tell that she expected me to laugh at her, tell her she was dreaming, or under the influence of a mysterious white powder that police on three continents would confiscate.

I allowed that it was certainly strange and then told her about Easter Eggs.

Since that time she's managed to find a way to have Windows 95 lose her desktop and replace every icon with unfamiliar icons labeled in Greek, although, from her description, it could have been Cyrillic. One interesting and malevolent switch on this one was that the code had some sort of time limit in it—after a couple of hours, everything came back by itself. I figure part of Mom's unflappability these days might be due to that particular joke. I've heard her say on a couple of occasions that things tend to work themselves out—something I can't say that I've ever noticed about computers in particular or life in general, for that matter. That particular knee-slapper also had the ugly side effect of filling the desktop up with extraneous copies of shortcuts, all of them hidden someplace off screen. I stumbled on that little fact when I was installing some new software about a month after the alphabet switch and had to spend an hour deleting 1109 copies of *New Folder*, *Qwicken* and *Ancient Empires*. You'd be amazed how long it takes to load the desktop with that many items on it.

Nowadays, Ma has taken to trying to track down these little glitches on her own and I kind of feel like a teacher whose star pupil has graduated. Proud, but a little nostalgic for the old days of dependency. I hadn't realized just how proud until a couple of weeks ago when she managed to figure out, on her own, how to use the Internet for long distance phone calls at cheap rates.

For about three weeks, we started getting these mysterious phone calls where there was no one on the line or we'd get a voice no one could recognize, punctuated by whistles and pops, mixed in with an echo. All of a sudden they went away and it wasn't but a day or so later that Mom told me she'd conquered the phone bill. When I asked how, she started to relate the particulars, only to stop and tell me she had just noticed she had a phone message. She dumped me to hold, checked her message and when she got back, informed me that Wilma, a close friend and fellow bridge club member, was having a dickens of a time with her computer.

I asked if she wanted me to give her a call and Ma said that I needn't bother right now. "This is only a level one alert," she replied. "If I can't fix it for her, then we can go to level two."

She didn't get back to me until the following day and when I asked, informed me primly that it was nothing. Wilma had just lost her desktop in Windows 95 and Mom fixed it for her. Not a problem.

Since that time, I don't get many calls from Ma asking for computer help.

I kind of miss them.

Stumps From Space

Properly speaking, this isn't my story to tell. It's my father's. However, I figure getting him to put something like this down on paper is about as difficult as kneecapping a centipede, which leaves the honor to me, since I've taken on the job of chronicling Toledo's slightly bent history.

This happened back in the early 70's when my father was principal of the Toledo Junior High School. The school year was winding down with only six or seven weeks to go before summer and by this time, the school had settled into a comfortable routine. That's why, I suppose, my father noticed something odd the minute it began. It was a Monday, and by third period, Dad had had reports from a number of teachers that there were several kids acting peculiar that morning. Dad decided to find out just what was going on, so he called a couple of the kids to the office to have a little chat.

The two kids, one boy and one girl, both lived out on Pioneer Mountain Road east of town, and claimed that nothing was wrong. Since twelve and thirteen year-old kids act squirrelly most of the time anyway, Dad chalked it up to nothing much and sent them back to class.

The following day, things seemed to be back to normal until my father discovered that one of the kids, the girl, I believe, hadn't showed up for school. Dad didn't have much more than a hunch to go on, and decided to let things stand as they were. Perhaps the girl was truly ill, he reasoned.

The next day, however, all of the kids my Dad had talked to now looked scared, and several of the teachers were concerned. Worse yet, one more kid who happened to live near the others on

Pioneer Mountain Loop, had come down with a case of the willies as well.

My Dad had still not decided what to do by the end of the second period, when one of the kids came to the office and asked if he could talk with Dad. The secretary ushered him into Dad's office; Dad sat him down and the kid blurted out the following story.

It seems that Monday night there were some strange lights on the north side of the mountain, and some strange sounds. The kid claimed he saw a space ship (a saucer—right?) come down out of the sky and land in a field not too far from his house.

At this point his story became rather confused—in any event it appeared that the kid's folks decided not to do anything but ignore it, hoping, I guess, it would go away. In point of fact, it did after a couple of hours.

The student said that the other kids had seen it too, but that it was gone in the morning—leaving only a big burned place in the field with the grass mashed down. The kids figured that if they told anybody about it, they be tagged as liars or loonies and besides, their parents told them they'd wallop the tar out of 'em if they talked about it at school. That was why they hadn't told my Dad the next day.

The next night nothing happened, and they figured they could just forget it. It turned out that the girl had been legitimately ill that day and there was no connection with the previous night visitors.

But the next night, the saucer came back and this time decided to see the sights, as it were. The kids described their "visitors" as little guys dressed in shiny suits, and one kid further related that the aliens started taking samples of various things they came across. Dad had the feeling the kid was somewhat relieved that the aliens didn't collect him or any of his pets.

Dad asked him what they had picked up and the kid said mostly plants, though they'd zapped one of the cows and taken the carcass into the ship. It was apparently at that point that his father had decided not to go on over and ask them for rent on the field they were using. He also said that they were, as of 7:00 a.m. that morning, still there. My Dad just looked at him for a bit, and then asked if he was sure.

Kid said yep, he was.

Dad called the other kids in one by one and got pretty much the same story—the fourth kid had only seen the ship the night before when the little aliens had waltzed over and taken some of the smaller livestock with them. He had seen them from about 100 feet away and claimed they looked like tree stumps with arms and legs.

My father is a fairly pragmatic man, and used to dealing with kids. He didn't doubt that there was something out of the ordinary going on, but he told me he figured that it was something the kids had gotten wrong somehow. He decided it needed a bit more investigating, so he called the local chief of police.

Now, I knew the chief of police in Toledo; he happened to be an old scuba diving buddy of mine, and a more unimaginative man you'd have to search hard to find. Jerry listened politely to my father, then asked what the hell was he supposed to do. Go out and arrest 'em?

No, Dad answered, just go out and see if everything's okay.

Right. So Jerry, not having a lot better to do right then, decided it wouldn't hurt to go on out and see for himself. Now a third individual comes into play. The local paper, The Lincoln Leader, had a staff of three people, one of whom got paid for writing stories—and it so happened that he was having coffee with the Chief at that time. Jerry asked if he'd like to come and the guy said, sure, why not?

Well, back at the school, the kid asked if it would be okay for his sister to pick him up—he was going to spend the rest of the week at her place there in town. He really didn't want to go back and see the aliens any more. Dad said sure, and let him call his sister.

About two hours later, Jerry showed up at the junior high and asked to see my Dad—unfortunately, Dad had had to go to a meeting and wasn't there, but the school secretary took the message. When my Dad got back, she commented that "Jerry looked kind of shook up." By this time, school was out so Dad decided to stop at City Hall and see just what was up.

The police chief and the journalist kept their date with infinity and trucked on out to Pioneer Mountain. Now if you know the Lincoln county area at all, you know that there aren't all that many flat spots in the Coast Range. Mostly it's made up of valleys with rather petulant looking hills surrounding. Rivers and creeks meander like all get out. In this particular area, there's a sheltered valley west of the mountain with about two or three acres of logged off land that is (or was at that time anyway) pasturage for the rather soggy critters that pass for cows in the area.

As I said, the cop and his reporter sidekick bopped out to the first house and got out of the squad car. Right off they could tell that something was not exactly typical Oregon Coast—no one came out and all dogs not in evidence. Usually you'll get inundated with two or three happy, but slobbery dogs, if you come up on a place around there, but not then. The field that was the most likely landing site was shielded from direct view from the driveway, so they started up a small access road to see if there really was a saucer there.

There was. Now you have to remember—this is at best second or third hand, depending on how you count these things. But I know Jerry. He said he saw a saucer. And there they were, walking tree stumps. Still picking up things here and there, and pointing funny looking objects at rather ordinary looking things.

I guess the police chief and the reporter just stood there looking at them for about thirty seconds or so, then approached a little closer till they were about twenty-five yards away from the nearest one—call it a hundred yards away from the ship. The reporter at that point suddenly remembered that he was a reporter and unlimbered the camera he had. As he raised it and began to focus, one of the "stumps" pointed a thingamajig at him and the camera went *ssswhip—crackle—zap*. Result, one dead camera, fused optics, the whole smear. The reporter never felt a thing. He just sort of stared dumbly at his now worthless camera.

Jerry, though not the swiftest bear in Lincoln county was, nevertheless, no damn fool, and he refrained from jumping up and down, screaming or even pulling his side arm.

Knowing Jerry, he might even have said something mild like, "Ah...jeez." The stump looked at the two of them for awhile, like he was daring them to try something else and then with a piney shrug, went back to what he had been doing, which was picking up leaves and twigs and stuffing them into a bag. The reporter and the cop watched a bit more. I guess they decided that nothing else was going to happen, show over and all that, so they turned around and went back to the police car, where they found the father and mother of the school kid looking at them from the now open door of the house.

The parents invited Jerry and the reporter in for something to drink, and I don't think it was coffee, though it could have been. The parents explained that it seemed that the best thing they could do was not cause a big fuss, and just sort of hang around the house while the stumps were out stumping around. After the one cow got sizzled, they hadn't had any problems with 'em, and they never did stay too long, so it seemed sort of polite like to just let them look around and leave them alone.

Safer, too.

Jerry and the reporter agreed. They finished their drinks and then Jerry and the reporter decided to call it a day and go home. And that's just about the end of the story.

The saucer went away and as far as I know, didn't come back again—though it's quite possible that it did and I just never heard about it. No one disappeared, except the reporter and that was due to him just plain bugging out. Jerry relayed the story to my dad, and left it at that.

One strange thing, though, was that when my dad told the story to a school principal from Siletz, the guy just shrugged and said it was the first time he'd ever heard of a saucer showing up that far south. According to him, they summered over in a secluded valley northwest of Siletz. Figure that out if you like.

Me, I don't try to.

Yard and Garden

Once in a while, somebody at work will start to describe some problem they're having at home with their yard and I'll have to beat a quick retreat to a neutral corner. I'm not liable to go berserk or anything—but I am liable to hyperventilate or twitch spasmodically, depending on how close it is to quitting time.

I hate yard work.

I don't *do* yard work.

That's what money is for. To hire somebody who *does* do yard work, preferably at some time when I'm not home. That was one of my earliest ambitions, never to have to mow another blade of grass, dig in another flower bed, argue with vegetation with the word poison in its name, or water anything that doesn't have four feet and move under its own power.

A few summers ago I had a close call, though. For a while, it looked as if I was going to have to do something about our yard. My wife, Susan, was about to throw in the towel and began to mutter something about Astroturf. I may have suggested that a couple of times in passing over the years, but the expense—my God! *Not* a good option. We could possibly afford paving it and then painting it green, but we'd have to dip into the kids' college fund to Astroturf.

It started out with a minor problem, a bit on the yuck side, I'll grant you, but not a big one. I was just about to have a Coke after moving the lawn furniture out onto the deck when I heard a sound best described as a shriek that morphed into a snarl. The sound came from the backyard.

I glanced around and spotted the dog lying quietly in the kitchen. It had to be Susan.

I looked outside surreptitiously and saw my wife standing in front of the main flowerbed, shaking her hands frantically and muttering Nevada outdoorsy-type curses. (Most seem to have to do with shooting something, don't ask me why.) She turned around and stomped into the house, her expression one of profound disgust. I memorized it. Something as perfect as that just has to be remembered.

I asked what was up and put some water on for tea, while I dug for my hearing aids. Irritated as she was, if she had something to say, I'd better be able to paraphrase what she said if I wanted to sleep in safety over the next week.

She muttered some things I didn't catch and then, when she saw me digging in the drawer, figured out the problem. She paused, and then boosted the gain as she grabbed a bottle of Wolfshead Ale. (Not a good sign). She washed her hands carefully, twice, and then told me, in detail.

Seems the ground she'd been preparing for violets and other annuals was in great shape, nice, moist, well wormed—whatever the hell that meant—and also crawling with thousands of pale, maggot-grub thingees, and did I know how it feels to grab a handful?

I figured it was a rhetorical question but you never know, so I replied words to the effect that it must have been...ah...disgusting?

Oh, yeah! Susan is not a person to go on at great length about most things but this one counted as a line drive into the stands. She groused for another five minutes, washed her hands a couple more times, finished her ale, and then got out the *gloves*.

At one time, the gloves had been white canvas, though you couldn't see any resemblance to canvas now. Suz only used them on serious projects involving noxious sprays, toxic powders, and poisonous grenades of imposing size. On the way back out the door, my youngest daughter called to her and came running up with a salad bowl full of dirt from the backyard.

Happily, Hilary informed her mother that the grubs were caddis flies, or would be if they were allowed to live out their normal life span. From the look on Susan's face, I didn't figure there was much chance of that. I'd put the odds at 6 to 1 on Susan.

For about two weeks, Suz did battle with the grubs. From her general demeanor, I figured things were at least progressing, even if she had not achieved total victory. For about a half-hour every other night, she'd don her gloves, lock up the cats and send the kids to the store to keep them from witnessing her commit eco-terrorism. As a member of PETA, the Sierra Club and the Joachim Miller Society, she really shouldn't be using chemicals that warn you to store them in a concrete bunker. She'd spray, turn over some dirt, mutter darkly for a few minutes and then come back into the house. I could tell it cost her—one cup of tea didn't cut it. Eventually, those caddis fly grubs with an itch to survive did a rush job of metamorphosing or bit the big one. End of crisis.

The next go-around lulled me to sleep. I mean, when one problem takes up that much time, the next problem to crop up isn't likely to be as taxing, at least from a resource point-of-view. Statistically speaking.

However, about the beginning of August that summer, I found Susan out in the backyard, talking to the expensive rose bush she'd purchased the year before and I figured we were on the downhill side. It would be a minor problem. Stood to reason.

Idiot notion, that. Big mistake. First off, Susan didn't continue to talk to the rose bush. Within a couple of days, she went from gentle chiding to furious ranting, all because the idiot plant refused to bloom on schedule. I don't want you to get the wrong idea about Susan; there's more to it than disgust with vegetative stubbornness or truth in plant advertising. Genuine concern prompted Susan to such extremes. This particular idiot plant hadn't bloomed at all that first summer, something that happens quite a lot with plants that have been stressed, if that's the word for it. Getting the bed all comfy for the roots takes time. However....

The plant isn't supposed to start blooming in December, which is what this particular rose did. Susan figured the damn thing was trying to commit a leafy version of seppuku, which may or may not have been correct. It's damn hard to pin motivation on a plant.

Anyway, Suz figured that if it didn't get to putting out the blossoms now, when it was supposed to, the damn thing'd be up all winter pumping out rose buds. End up killing itself by dint of overwork and bad timing. That didn't fit with Susan's game plan for the yard.

I mentioned that verbal threats didn't really seem to be effective against plants, but she just looked at me darkly, muttered something about evolutionary pressure and went back to describing how she'd uproot the sucker and feed it to a chipper if it didn't shape up.

Up until this point in my life, I'd always figured that members of the plant kingdom had zip for sentience. I more or less wrote the bugger off and figured we'd have to dig its carcass out of the flower bed sometime around March, or perhaps April at the latest. The lack of ears alone looked like an insurmountable handicap.

Susan, herself, seemed to lose heart before two weeks had passed. I expected her to retire the plant permanently, only to discover one day that the little blighter had actually managed to put forth five or six hastily grown bud facsimiles. I wouldn't call it a full bloom by any stretch of the imagination, but it had to be counted as an honest effort.

But it puzzled me. What had worked? I mean, how did Susan get the message across? I finally couldn't stand it any more and asked her point-blank. "How did you do it?"

Susan gave me one of those infuriating, small smiles all spouses see from time to time when they've asked a question that stands only a ten percent chance of getting answered. After an inordinate amount of coaxing and jollying, she finally broke down and took me out to look at the rose bush. She pointed at a number of sticks that poked up, here and there around the plant, ringing it in a vaguely threatening way. She explained they were from the climbing rose out front—stuff so old that it had died and she'd been forced to prune it back to encourage new growth.

I must have muttered something out loud to the effect that I still didn't see a connection. She looked at me pityingly and then at the rose bush, and then back at me. Apparently Rosie and I had more in common than I'd have thought. She merely said, "Object lesson." With that, she gathered up the tools of her trade and went into the other yard to sit in the sun, drink tea and read.

At that point, I nodded to myself and reflected that I would, in the future, see if I could avoid any Object Lessons Susan might want to toss my way. If a plant is smart enough to know when it's licked, surely I could learn a thing or two from it. And I've more-or-less kept that in the back of my mind ever since.

I can't say as I hate gardening now, so much as I fear it. She's got all those cutting tools.

Take a Left

My wife and I have an alliance against the rest of the world when it comes to that tired old observation that men either won't or can't ask for directions. We flip a quarter and the loser gets to do the onerous task. Until my wife cops to the fact that I have fast fingers and a double headed quarter, we'll keep doing it that way, too.

Actually, I think she knows, but is too nice to make an issue of it, even though she has the same feeling about the process that I do. We both got that way because of the same rather unpleasant experience, having to do with finding a place called Janzen Beach. It certainly put a mark on me, at any rate.

We were living on the coast with my folks, and by the time August rolled around we were getting bored and wanted to do something out of the ordinary—if you ever feel this way, take a deep breath and rethink whatever pops into your head. I think there's a psychic facility in people that takes that vague, diffuse feeling and roots around in the ether to satisfy that itch. What you end up with will definitely be extraordinary, but tends to be just the shy side of lunacy, over the line into impossible, or both, with a strong aspect of unpleasant.

What we came up with was visiting Portland for shopping, dinner, and a visit to an amusement park at Janzen Beach. The first went fine, if you like shopping which I don't.

The second had a couple of hitches in it, but we managed okay, all things considered. Mom and Susan decided on a Japanese restaurant and so we had to take off our shoes and sit on the floor. I do that regularly anyway, sitting cross-legged, but Mom, Dad, and Susan don't and my father spent an uncomfortable fifteen minutes until he found by accident that there was a hidden recess under the table where western persuasion guests could park their feet. The food was good and the drinks stealthy, both in price and effect. When it came time to leave, Mom and Susan made the rude discovery of Newton's Fourth Law of Feet: Walk three miles in shopping malls, take your shoes off and your feet swell like Ball Park Franks on a hot barbecue. Fortunately, the drinks had started to take effect by that time, numbing their feet and giggling their heads, so when we left, they only limped a tiny bit.

The next stop was to be the Janzen Beach Amusement Park, which is near the Columbia River in the north section of Portland. I drove, Mom giving directions I didn't need, to find Interstate 5. Once we crossed the Willamette and got into Northeast Portland I figured we'd have no problem. It was 8 p.m. or thereabouts.

Soon, I caught sight of a ferris wheel and began to look for the Janzen Beach exit. I started getting concerned when the lights of the park started to slip into the night behind us and I'd still not seen any exit. I asked my three copilots to keep a sharp eye out and within three or four minutes, Susan pointed out the sign to Janzen Beach.

I looked in the rear view mirror and shook my head. We had to be three miles away from the park if my eyes could be believed, and I wondered why they had the exit so far away.

Did you notice a progression with the first two? Keep that thought.

I took the exit, crossed under the freeway and looked for signs, only there weren't any signs to the park. Okay, I thought— you can see the sucker, try getting to it that way. We took the first street with a stop light and turned south. The road curved to the west after some twists and turns, and I started looking for another southern route.

No sweat. One offered itself and I took it, noting that the ferris wheel was noticeably closer. I was still smiling smugly to myself when we wandered into an industrial park, festooned with quartz halogen security lights, looming black shapes of terminal cranes and dump trucks, and stacks of busted up wooden pallets. After a set of corkscrew turns that ran between warehouses, machine shops, and spooky looking power sub-stations, my father remarked that we seemed to be lost.

Thanks, Dad.

I tried to retrace our route—not a good idea—we should have been sending up Beri Flares at that point—all the while, we kept getting further and further away from the Park. We could see it, but we just couldn't get there from wherever the hell we were. After twenty minutes of driving aimlessly, we parked and discussed the problem; the discussion consisting of curses from me, occasional giggles from Mom and Susan, and grumpy grousing from my father. We would have had to wait for a search party to find us if a local cop hadn't driven by. We must not have looked suspicious because he rolled on by without stopping.

I didn't let our chance get away. I pulled out and followed the cop, hoping that he'd lead us to some part of town that didn't have a law against road signs. It eventually worked, but we got to see most of the industry camped out in Portland before we were done. I swear the cop knew what was going on and intentionally gave us the nickel tour.

He finally lost us near a huge shopping center that had closed for the evening. I parked the car and we got down to the proper business of assigning blame. Once that was done, we all felt better and started discussing what we should do. I was all for canning it in, but I got overruled, and after a moment or so, the ugly phrase, "Ask for Directions," naturally came up.

I can't see the ferris wheel anymore...

Yard and Garden

Mom pointed out that there was an all-night gas station on the other side of the parking lot, and against my better judgment, I drove over and rolled the window down.

The attendant was a thin, wiry guy with a doleful expression, and I asked him how to get to Janzen Beach. I was informed I was at Janzen Beach.

At that point, I figured Janzen Beach had to be a hell of a lot bigger than I'd reckoned. I politely nodded and popped the question: "How do I get to the Janzen Beach Amusement Park?"

At that point, Mr. Thin and Wiry cracked up and called out to a friend working on a truck up on a rack.

"Hey, Mark. This guy's looking for Janzen...Beach...Amusement...Park!" Thereupon, the other guy cracked up as well.

Thin and Wiry struggled to contain himself, and after nearly choking on his own drool, managed to tell me that the amusement park had been torn down ten years ago. To put in a shopping center. This particular shopping center, to be precise.

"But what about the ferris wheel?" I asked. I could see it, plain as day, not more than a mile away. In-between guffaws, he managed to choke out that what I was looking at was the Multnomah County Fair, and just what rock had I been hiding under, anyway?

I rolled the window back up and left, a valuable lesson learned. Asking for directions will only get you where you want to go if the place you want to go is in the same time zone and doesn't have a double.

All in all, this particular humiliation didn't scar me for life, though it did leave a lingering effect. Being relatively experienced with looking like a cretin out for a stroll during a typhoon, my skin has gotten a bit thicker; however, I have a secret conviction that coincidences are anything but random. Consequently, anytime somebody drops an observation that there's little chance of some horrible event taking place, I immediately start figuring how far away I want to be when it does happen. I'm fairly confident that luck plays only a tiny role in disaster and humiliation.

My kind of luck, anyway.

What To Do In Boardman When Your Pickup Up And Dies

I've written about my abilities as a mechanic before, so it shouldn't come as any great shock that I've been forced over the years to come up with contingency plans, should some mechanical or electrical doohickey hiccup and keel over. I suspect most people do to some extent, but probably don't have plans for every eventuality. I know I don't.

A case in point would be my last trip to the wilds of Eastern Oregon.

I work for the Oregon Department of Transportation as an analyst, and end up looking at projects throughout the state with the exclusion of the Portland/Metro area (Thank God for a gentleman named Merle, who does that). This particular time I was headed for the town of Baker, Oregon, or, as the citizens of the town decided a few years ago, Baker City, which is in the northeast quarter of the state.

There are several ways to get there, particularly if you don't mind taking a long time to do it, which I do. So I elected to follow I-84 across the top of the state, and drop down into Baker City from the northwest. Since about 90% of the traffic to and from Baker does that, you couldn't really say I was sneaking up on the town.

My faithful pickup, a '96 Nissan, had been getting creaky over the last year, which was to be expected when you've managed to put 88,000 miles on the beast with minimal automotive maintenance. My wife, Susan, had suggested that I not take the pickup, but use a state owned rig, instead. She reasoned that if a state car died on me, the state would be forced to send somebody out to gather up the pieces—which would most likely include me—and she could sleep easier that night.

I told her I figured the pickup could handle just one more long trip before needing more repairs, and got set up to leave the next day. (At this point, you probably should mentally add background music from *Jaws*.) By about 2 p.m. I had already tootled through The Dalles, Rufus Junction, the Columbia River Gorge, and had started into the plains which stretch threateningly eastward toward Pendleton. The scenery isn't much, I'm afraid, just brown grass, brown, black and gray colored rocks, and brown sky due to the wind which blows 93% of the time at just under gale force. (There's a reason why ODOT has signs along this stretch of roadway that say *Wind Gusts, Dust* and *Expect Falling Houses*.)

I was keeping a steady pace of about 65 when I heard a tremendous thud/crash kind of sound, followed by the engine strangling itself dramatically with a consequent and alarming loss of speed. You can imagine my surprise at this, since I happen to be stone deaf. I don't hear many things these days.

Fortunately, I have razor quick reactions, and was able to get my five or six curses said before I had to deal with crossing a lane of traffic to reach the outside shoulder. That's where I slowly rolled to a stop. I figured I was about ten miles west of the Boardman interchange, which was hardly good news, since I wasn't sure that Boardman had phones, let alone mechanics and tow trucks.

In most of the bizarre classes they show students learning to drive, other than the obligatory hamburger highway film extravaganza, they always emphasize how one signals to passing motorists that one's vehicle is *kaput*, and that one could use a lift. I noted that I lacked the required white handkerchief, but then, as I looked at the hood of my pickup, I reflected that the white handkerchief didn't matter a lot, inasmuch as I also lacked a radio antenna to tie it to. I did have a hood to raise, however, so I did.

Batting 33% like that, I figured I'd probably make Baker sometime in the next week.

I went through my packed clothes and was able to find a mismatched pair of white socks and some twine, so I made an ersatz white, surrender flag. I never did figure out a good replacement for the radio antenna. I tried tying it to various parts of the car, but none of them seemed to beckon any passing motorists with any degree of success.

I looked the situation over, stared at the cars whizzing by, and came to the conclusion that I'd have to be a bit more specific in my request for aid. I dug through my computer bag, grabbed a black marker I use as part of the AC adapter then took out a file folder and carefully printed in highly legible, eight inch, pleading letters, **HELP**.

As you will note, I had boiled down my entire message into something that someone driving by at 70 or 80 mph could read.

With a little ingenuity, I managed to post my request on the back window of my pickup and then started rummaging around to get my gear packed up and ready to go when somebody stopped to **HELP**.

I watched the traffic for awhile. After a few minutes of that, my trained, analytic eyes spotted something. The only effect my sign had, was that people in the outside lane changed lanes, to give me a wider berth when they zoomed by me. I debated whether or not to try looking forlorn and desperate, but I figured the best I could manage would be to look pissed-off and unstable.

What To Do In Boardman When Your Pickup Up And Dies

Still, I decided to give it some time, and after an hour, figured that the one police car that passed without stopping or slowing down should be taken as a sign that this was not working.

I decided to leave my overnight bag, grab my computer stuff and a few other things and head off down the highway in search of Boardman. I also left a note for anyone who happened by which explained that I had left to get a tow truck. I then took down my **HELP** sign figuring it might be mistaken by some as a **HELP YOURSELF** sign.

I covered a mile before a gentleman in a full sized pickup pulled over to ask if I needed **HELP**. My sign worked like one of those old naval flags signaling Black Death riding in first class, yet my ambling along the shoulder of the interstate got a quick inquiry regarding my need for aid. Go figure.

I gratefully accepted, and after twenty minutes found myself in Boardman, Oregon, looking for a tow truck and a garage. I quickly found both, got out my Triple A card, and within forty-five minutes had my poor Nissan sitting in the back of a garage with a mechanic looking at it.

Going deaf has taken a bit of getting used to, but I have to admit it's done wonders for my mental flexibility. I can repeat out loud, my best guess at what's being said faster than a chipmunk on methamphetamine. It turned out that I needn't have worried; the guy who ran the place had one of those carefully arranged minds one hears about, and hopefully, doesn't antagonize too often. He wrote that the engine was blown.

I read that, and figuring that this was not a good place for experimental communication, asked him just what he meant by blown. He looked at me for a moment, pointed first at my pickup and then at the repair estimate, before he wadded up the estimate and with a broad grin, flipped it into the trash can twelve feet away.

I really didn't need a translator.

After a bit of writing and talking back and forth, I left my pickup parked behind the garage and forlornly walked over to a motel sitting just south of the interchange. I got myself a room and tried to figure out my next move. It took me a bit of time, but I finally managed to coax my wife into coming to the motel that night to pick me up. At this point I should say that Susan wouldn't arrive till sometime after midnight—when she once again proved how deep-down nice and scrupulously fair she really is. She only once told me *I-told-you-so*. I can't begrudge that; she was right.

I had a lot of free time on my hands until she arrived. I figured that if I was lucky, I could kill a full half hour sightseeing in Boardman itself, but that still left me with at least four hours of dead time. I hadn't brought any books with me, unfortunately, so reading wasn't an option unless I found something to read. I decided the motel owner could direct me to the closest supermarket which would have books and magazines, so I dropped by the motel office.

The motel owner, a woman of about sixty wearing a pullover yellow and white striped shirt with a dead alligator over the pocket, rubbed her nose for a couple of seconds, reflecting. She then indicated with pointing and ultimately a bit of shoving, that there was a market to the south about a quarter mile away and I started walking.

I noticed there was a walkway to the market, though it turned out to be a trifle odd. It started up at the edge of the Suds 'n Wash Auto Centre and diverged from the roadway itself, until there was a ten-foot gap of scrubby grass between the asphalt walkway and the roadway. At that point a low white fence began, almost as if pedestrians had become a threatened species that needed protection. The walkway even had cute little stop bars on it at each road and driveway crossing for those walkers who might be unclear on the concept of right-of-way.

What To Do In Boardman When Your Pickup Up And Dies

I got some provisions and something to read before I headed back to the motel, getting there about the time it got dark, still somewhat bemused by the care shown to the lowly pedestrian.

Even though it didn't appear that I'd get a chance to actually walk through the heart of Boardman, I next perused the motel travel and tourist information sheet in the room. I discovered that the number one activity from the little list of things-to-do was a visit to a new marina on the Columbia which had the added attraction of, and this is a direct quote, "...a modern, paved walkway" that apparently ran the length of the marina and..."*beyond.*"

The map indicated that the "*beyond*" was five or six hundred feet long and dead-ended in a cul-de-sac sporting what the map legend identified as a trash receptacle. The next most highly regarded activity was to admire the Columbia River, possibly from some point on the walkway, though the list didn't actually say that.

That was the entire list.

I plan to take time off sometime and revisit Boardman, now that I know what to do in Boardman when your pickup up and dies. I'll make sure to wear comfortable walking shoes, and I'll walk both the marina and the "*beyond,*" and then around town. I may even look for the guy who forgot to add downtown Boardman to the list—he really should add it.

After all, you need at least three things before you have a list.

Kettle Coppers

You probably don't know it, but the Salvation Army is far more than it seems. Over the last few weeks, I've discovered evidence that within that supposedly charitable organization exists a cadre of people pulling strings and following a malignant plan the outside world knows nothing of. Indeed, after hours and hours of research, digging into records and intelligence gathering, I've only scratched the surface. I dread what other horrors I'd uncover, should I continue.

I speak of nothing short of a secret enemies list kept by the Salvation Army. It's hardly surprising when the clues are laid out in front of you. Even the name is a subterfuge. What is the abbreviation of Salvation Army? SA, of course. And where have we seen those letters before, I ask you?

Nazi Germany.

There's more.

I first became aware that something wasn't kosher right after Thanksgiving. That's when the SA starts their public activities. By now, no one thinks twice when they see a man or woman standing at the entrance of a business, the red kettle hanging in front or beside them, the small bell clanging a complicated subliminal beat that physiological psychologists would be studying in detail, if funding could be found. It won't ever be, of course. The SA will never allow it.

In the past, I've generally put a buck or two in the kettle each time I encounter one, always on the way out of whatever business I'm visiting. I cash a check for over the amount so I'll have something to pitch in since it's tax deductible—and that's the key to their heinous plan.

The first time this year, the SA rep was a sawed-off, chunky guy with brush cut, white hair and reading glasses. He had watery blue eyes, a Santa hat, and that benign smile they all have. He muttered something about Merry Christmas and I answered with the incorrect ritual response. Instead of Happy Holidays or Season's Greetings, I muttered "What aisle is it on?" as I went by. That was all it took.

(Memo: Check out Hallmark! 81.3% of their Christmas cards have Season's Greeting on them, somewhere. I suspect collusion.)

Behind my back, Santa's Helper took out his cell phone, noted my description and had me tailed. This would allow them to identify me, as well as time what happened next. The second I finished paying for my groceries, the SA operative picked up and left. I know they have a video of me walking by on the way in and not donating anything. Once I emerged from the store, they took a video of me looking around and finally going back to my car, my donation still in hand. Once the IRS sees those tapes, I'm cooked.

Once I was identified and placed on the list, all they had to do the next time was bounce sound waves from the bell off me, compare the reflected waves against a database of known enemies, and bingo—they know they have a target. I've never caught one of them in the act of picking up, so they must keep the target under surveillance inside. Their timing is superb. Again and again, the pattern repeats itself. In front of Rite-Aid, B. Dalton's. Thriftway—numerous times at Thriftway because I drop in two or three times a day. My God, even in front of the US Post Office. There, they're particularly adroit. You go in, they leave. You come out, they're nowhere to be seen. You drive away, they get back into position. Don't be fooled, the US Postal Service, which surely must be in cahoots with them, is a quasi-corporation—and it's as efficient as a heat pump when it wants to be.

Ho Ho Ho

They're shrewd. Very, very shrewd. Once in a while, on some random basis that even the computer from *2001* couldn't decode, they stay and wait for me to come out. It's rare—less than 5% of the time—but it lulls suspicion and gives them a chance to plant bugs in my packages while I fumble with my wallet.

Check. You'll see. If you're on their list, you'll find not one, but two slips of paper. The second is a cleverly camouflaged listening device that looks like a coupon or a "Tell Us How We're Doing!" card.

What can you do? That depends entirely upon whether or not you're already on the enemies list. If you are *not* on the list, you're better off not to fight it. When somebody greets you with Merry Christmas or Happy Hanukkah, Season's Greetings or Happy Holidays, you *must* respond in kind. In fact, to be safe, you should treat any such greeting as the threat it is and respond instantly. Silence, or a reply of "Only if I want to," won't cut it.

If you've discovered slips of paper in your bags that aren't receipts, you're on the list. Your options are nonexistent, I'm afraid.

Late last night, one option finally occurred to me. I haven't tried it yet because once thwarted, like any wounded, rabid beast, the Salvation Army is unpredictable and very dangerous to cross. Physical violence is a distinct possibility. Anyone who wants to fight back should first check the obituary records of Salem, Oregon for mine. If I'm there...well...you're on your own.

My wife says I have a black sense of humor and I suppose she's right. With the threat of violence as likely as it is, I've decided the only fitting place to try my plan is at the post office, where violence is no new thing. Bystanders shouldn't be shocked too much.

I'll make a donation *before* I go inside. I just hope I don't take anybody else down with me.

War of Wits

Our family is what you might call an extended family, but wouldn't if you had speciesist leanings. We consist of a mother (by design), a father (of sorts—I have no training you see), one teenager (still no training), and a kid (one who demanded both training and design—don't ask) plus five cats (various pedigrees and admixtures) and a dog (a pedigree Samoyed). I'm not sure it could be called a typical American family, even if you stretch the concept. I am sure that this is what would be called, for want of a better term, a thinking, witty family, barring only myself, of course, since I am, by all accounts around me, relatively witless. Surely clueless.

The cats, for example, have a constant war of wits going and it's an interesting diversion from Kosovo and the Oregon Legislature. Of the five cats, three are indoor and two are indoor-outdoor models. There's a weird kind of hierarchy generated by that; it's one that sociologists might call something like mutually dominant, self-reinforced and Dionysian. Which just means that all five cats figure that their side's better than the other; they don't encourage talking with the enemy; and they fight like hell on it. Then there's the split between reality oriented and reality impaired. Again, we're talking a three and two split fortunately, and this one has the charming quality of being a scream to watch—the reality impaired ones anyway.

Sam is a coal-black, yellow-eyed, mini-panther of a kitty, and his problem might simply be poor eyesight, coupled with a kitten-like sense of wonder. No box is too small for him to get into. Ask him. My oldest daughter Cassie claims him and carries him around in her arms occasionally, to which he responses by staring at the ceiling like he's never seen one before. At least, not up close enough to actually see. I tested that idea out by picking him up and walking with him in my arms, and yep, he looks at everything he normally can't see with an astonished air.

The second is a long hair American Curl we got from the pound (along with Sam and one other), who is skittish as hell, paranoid, and suffers from short term memory problems. When we first got him, he couldn't recollect how the house was arranged, after each nap. Finding the litter box or the food meant major exploration. Everybody who left the house for more than an hour or two became total strangers upon their reentry. It made for weird encounters, because sometimes, just staying in the bathroom long enough for a bath and shave, might put you over his time limit.

He's improved. Up until a year or so ago, we had made major progress; people could be gone for a day or two and he could still remember them. Then he relapsed when we went on a trip to Gold Beach without him. We left him and the others with a house sitter, and consequently had to reintroduce ourselves when we came home. His memory retention is now about as long as it was before we left.

His name is Claude, by the way. Claude, as in that poor, nervous, yellow cat in the Warner Brothers cartoons that the two mice drive to the brink of a nervous breakdown. We had no trouble naming him.

There's another war of wits going on in the house, only this one is not species specific. My wife and her dog, Nikki, have tussles over food—what else do dogs care about?

Nikki is a thief. Chocolate, for example, is always in season, even though he runs severe risks if he has any—as all dogs do, of course. Then there's the concept of leftovers. All leftovers, doggie-bag or not, are by natural law, his. I hadn't realized the law had changed on that. I was laboring under the delusion that we were still under the Ground Level rule, which states that anything

that hits the floor is legitimately the dog's. Nikki showed me the fine print on his pedigree, and by God, the dog's right.

My wife, however, refuses to accept the new accords, and operates under the provisions of the Nevada Legislature's 1931 law that states leftovers may and should be eaten by the owner within two days or risk forfeiture to the nearest convenient pet. I, showing some low animal cunning of my own, switch sides at every opportunity, fan the fires, and laugh like hell. Don't condemn me out-of-hand; it still beats, is more honest, and is in much better taste than anything the World Wrestling Federation delivers.

Susan quickly learned that leaving any white box of leftovers in the car alone with the dog was much like throwing in the towel. He'd open the box, eat the contents and jadedly move back to the fourth seat (we have an APV) to munch the box. She next tried to leave the box shoved way up under the front windshield—the dash is about two and a half feet wide with a really acute angle between the glass and the dashboard. A person has to really stretch to retrieve things from there.

Not even a challenge. I don't know how the hell he does it, but he does. Susan's trick has never worked to my knowledge.

She tried shoving the white box of leftovers into the glove compartment, but that only takes very small boxes and it turns out Nikki can work latches. That took him a bit of trying and a number of attempts but he mastered it fairly quickly.

Next, Susan tried locking things in an Igloo ice/lunch box. You know, the ones with the button on one end you have to press to swivel the top off? That stumped him. He never did defeat that. However he re-leveled the playing field by the simple trick of hiding the Igloo. Nobody will claim doing it, but the box gets put back into the garage all of the time and unless Susan checks before we leave, we generally end up with it back there, us sitting in a parking lot, and one doggie bag in dire jeopardy of one doggie.

Normally, Susan is a woman of calm and even temperament, and she takes this maneuver in the spirit of which it's performed. She curses. Particularly if we've got Chinese take-out. But I have to admit, Susan is no quitter. She developed a counter that's perfect and unfair as all get out. She locks the dog in the car, and either takes the food with her or, more frequently now to provide a bit of fairness, sets the box under the car. Once in a while, she drives off forgetting it and they both lose, but not usually.

I asked her once why she thought that was fairer than taking it with her. Or eating all of the food before we left the restaurant. Her reply was illuminating and shows the wonderful sport my wife actually is. She told me that if he can figure out which button to hit to unlock the car, and develops an opposable thumb to grab the door handle and pull, he can have the box.

Provided, of course, he can find it under the car. What could be fairer than that?

Do not, repeat, *do not*, play Monopoly with this woman. Not if she can afford hotels.

The Hose that Wouldn't Die

I was home sick a couple of days ago and happened to be around when my wife pulled out her magic plastic bags of pantyhose. I took the opportunity to ask her if she was still getting the stuff through the mail. She looked a bit sheepish, possibly due to the fact that over the years, she's made mention of the fact that she probably has enough pantyhose stuffed into her closet to keep a platoon of cross-dressing NFL football quarterbacks in pantyhose till hell cracks.

She admitted she did still get them and looked a bit defiant. Not being either stupid or without a soft spot in my heart for anything that comes in the mail, I ventured I thought it was nice she did, but confessed confusion—she had, after all, written them and asked them to stop sending pantyhose. I could distinctly remember several such letters being penned.

Perhaps I'd better back up a bit and fill in some background.

Susan, my wife, has been getting pantyhose in the mail for going on twenty-five years. I don't recall how she got started with The Company (which I can't name simply because I don't KNOW the name), but she came to the startling revelation about fifteen years ago that she had more pantyhose than she was ever likely to need. That's assuming she would be wearing pantyhose five days a week for the rest of her life, and calculating that she lives to be something like 95 and a half years old. That's kind of an optimistic forecast, if you ask me, since I can't see her voluntarily wearing them all that often once she takes to tootling around in a wheelchair powered by a small fusion reactor. (I'm looking forward to driving one of those myself, by the way).

Over the next five or six years, she put in a running battle with The Company, writing letters asking them to stop sending the packages to her, or at least, to slow them down some. At one point I think she asked for a court ordered cooling off period, similar to what the courts do for dead-in-the-water labor contract negotiations. In any event, they kept coming, always with a nice note apologizing for bothering her and she kept paying for them. She told me at one point, "They're really the finest pantyhose you can buy. In fact, they're too good."

That caught my attention. I asked for a bit of explanation, since I found it hard to believe that there could be all that much difference between brands of pantyhose. She looked at me with that look she reserves for whenever I've inadvertently shown I can't be trusted with more than a buck and a half at one time. She patiently sat me down and explained the ins and outs of pantyhose, which took ten minutes. I probably should have been taking notes, but at the time, I didn't realize that there would be a test later on.

I was informed that pantyhose comes in only a few sizes and that bad pantyhose all come in the same three sizes that fit no one known in the western world. These are too small, way too small, and big enough for elephants.

Then there's the fact that the knees aren't where the knees are supposed to be, sometimes appearing on the side of the leg, but more often sitting up or down about six inches from where the average female is likely to have knees. Pantyhose that have knees to the side are considered collector's items, I guess, and Susan has a tiny, but nice collection of them hidden high in the closet where they're safe. None of them, by the way, are from The Company. Then there are the ones that have mismatched feet, where one foot, size 0, is in one position and the other, size 18 EEE, is rotated about thirty degrees port or starboard, thus giving the hose a twist around one leg that cuts off blood flow precisely by 1:30 p.m. every day that they're worn.

Then there are those that come from the factory with runs. Really cheap pantyhose will be carefully pre-run, as it were. During the 1990's, when the modern management fads hit full stride, this particular flaw was touted as a sign of power-pantyhose, since they wasted less time. The run was already in, and the wearer could move on to more important duties. Again, none of the pantyhose from The Company had runs.

The sizes The Company had were perfect and fit everybody. They had one small and stretchy that would fit cute Munchkin women, to one that would work for Wagnerian Opera singers. There probably wasn't a woman in the world, including French women who hadn't shaved their legs since D-Day, who couldn't find one size/type that fit them. They even had a handout that would help the person find the right size for them. Susan looked at the handout once when she'd first started buying the brand and had no need to see it since.

They were tough. They lasted. They wore well. They came in a spectrum of shades from clear to dense black, tight weave to mesh. They couldn't apparently be harmed by any detergent known to humanity, and probably would have been useful protecting women who had to contend with radioactive fallout. Those women who wore pantyhose from The Company and lived near Love Canal had been shown to have cancer rates only a quarter the rate of non-Company wearing women. If anything, they were the perfect pantyhose. They never, ever, ran.

In point of fact, such perfection was the problem. What truly marks this particular brand of pantyhose as superior is that they apparently don't run on their own, at all. They don't even run when worn. I asked for a bit of clarification, thinking perhaps I misunderstood and that these hose prevented rapid leg movement, entirely. That, I'd think, wouldn't be too big a selling point to anyone who depended upon public transportation. No, I was told, these pantyhose never got a run in them. Ever. Susan grabbed one, went to the bathroom and came back with a pair of scissors and showed me.

She couldn't give them a run. Susan tried determinedly, but just couldn't do it. I expressed amazement, probably a little less than I should have since this is a remarkable property of any hose, it turns out.

Susan then said, and I quote, "They don't run; they don't rip; and they don't wear out." She grabbed a big sack from her closet and upended it on the bed, nearly smothering two of our cats. "I've worn all of these at least two or three times. Some as many as twenty or thirty."

I began to get the picture. "So," I said, "You don't really need to buy any more, then. Right?"

Susan looked at me and said words to the effect that no female descendant of hers in the next hundred years was ever going to need to buy pantyhose. She started to stuff them back into the bag.

I thought about it and then had to ask, "Didn't you get them to stop sending them? I thought you did." Susan nodded and continued to stuff pantyhose back into her sacks. "So, how come you're getting them now? Did they talk you into it?" Susan again nodded. She looked a bit defiant and chagrined at the same time. She also looked a bit sad. "So why?"

She sat down on the bed before she answered. "Well, a couple of reasons. First off, I really like The Company. They're such nice people. I've talked to a couple of the reps a number of times and they're neat. Had a good time talking to them. Second, they kind of begged me to continue. It was hard to turn my back on them after so many years. I mean, they stood by us when we were just starting out and I had trouble paying for them. I'd miss a month or two and they never said anything, ever."

"Nice people," I said.

There is only
one logical answer.

We buy another closet.

She nodded. "And one of them pointed out that if I stopped buying them, it would be a bit like punishing them for making a product too well. I certainly didn't want to do that." I nodded. I had to agree with her. "So, I talked them into cutting down on the number they sent and started taking them again. It seemed like the only decent thing to do." I had to agree with her but I also had one worry that I couldn't shake. "But how are we going to find a place for them? I mean, look at your closet. It's stuffed. There's hardly any room left at all."

Susan shrugged and then got up and opened my closet, reached back and pulled out a dark green, heavy plastic bag that had a cord fixed to the rim, held it up for a moment, and then stuffed it back in the upper left corner. She added a second bag beside. The same bag she'd opened up and dumped on the bed. "You don't mind, do you?"

I thought a moment and then shook my head. "Not as long as 1: you don't ask me to wear them and 2: they don't leap out of the closet at me, anytime soon."

So far so good. The overflow is sitting patiently in my closet as I type this right now. That's another nice thing about this brand of pantyhose. They're very well behaved. One might even say polite.

Food Fascism

I don't usually make an issue of the food I eat, but then again, that's probably because those around me know exactly what I will and will not shove toward my stomach, via the esophagus. That reluctance is partly due to a overwhelmingly stubborn nature, but also to a variety of experiences that I wouldn't wish on Tupac Shakur or any other number of rap/hip hop stars who have attitude problems. That wonderful pastime called eating has been an eclectic mix of fun, fear and force since I was just a tyke.

My attitudes on food are primarily the result of domestic excursions into the culinary arts, though some of the institutional memories I have are pretty potent, too. I think the fact that my own loving family would do some of the things that they did...well, it's hard. Your family is supposed to be on your side.

My earliest excursion in food fascism came when my sister and I were sent to stay for a few days with my Uncle Keith and Aunt Shirley. I don't remember the occasion that called my folks away, but it apparently was unsuitable for youngsters, else I'm sure they'd have taken us. Imposing on my father's brother and sister-in-law with what the rest of the Browning family called *that kid*, called in a lot of debts, carefully stored away for the future.

I think I was four or five.

My uncle and I didn't go head to head until supper the second night, when my aunt announced that we'd have a treat for dinner. I had already tumbled to the fact that grownups trying to put something over on kids affected a bluff, hearty tone of voice. I figured I was doomed. My uncle chimed in at that point and revealed that the treat would be corn fritters and syrup.

I immediately wanted to know what a corn fritter was.

Feeding time in the
Browning household

My uncle informed me, grandly, that it was a type of pancake with corn inside.

I kept an eye on my aunt while she made dinner, and with a sinking feeling, saw that she didn't use fresh or frozen corn; she used canned corn. That was going to be a problem. The last three times I'd been coaxed into eating canned corn, my stomach had coaxed the corn right back out. Longest it had stayed inside my stomach was about fifteen seconds.

You can guess the rest. We sat down. My uncle assigned my sister and I two corn fritters, each. I bleakly reported that in all likelihood I'd throw up. My uncle said to eat it anyway. So I did.

Once my prophecy had been fulfilled, we proceeded to clean up the table. I trace the rather cold relationship between my uncle and myself from that time.

Surprisingly, the weird foods and food additives my mother foisted off on me never seemed to cause hard feelings from my point of view. I suppose I realized early on that Ma really was just trying to make things more interesting and healthful for my father, sister and I. Granted, interesting is kind of a bland way to describe Tiger's Milk, a wheat germ derivative that we normally chugged down in orange juice. That was about the same time we were also taking brewer's yeast in small brick-shaped tablets, Nutrobio health pills by the handful and soy products. I'm lucky I didn't ferment.

That finally culminated with an exotic food phase that might have been triggered by a trip to Portland when I was six. We happened to stop at a couple of places that dealt in exotic food. I don't specifically recall noticing Mom picking up any canned goods, something my sister and I had learned was generally not a good sign.

My best guess is that she purchased all the stuff and had it shipped to us in Prineville. That would be the sort of sly, crafty thing Mom would come up with, knowing our attitude. All I know for sure is that one afternoon in March, I was digging around in the cupboard for some graham crackers and marshmallow spread and happened to find a whole bunch of canned foods hidden behind a sack of rice and a sack of kidney beans.

I asked Mom about it because, although I could read pretty well by that time, I had trouble reading the labels and wondered what the stuff was. I suppose I should have tumbled to something sinister when Ma told me that she couldn't read the labels either. While that made a certain amount of sense for some of the labels, a couple of them were in French and I knew Ma taught French. Ma was up to something and like a victim in a horror flick, I just had to know more. I was forced to go by whatever pictures were on the can.

To this day, I'm not sure what some of the stuff was. I'm not sure I *want* to know what some of that stuff was. Those that I do remember having choked down were bad enough, particularly when Dad sourly identified the food group for my sister and I, but not the food.

There was, and I am *not* making this up, a can of Reindeer Meatballs. That certainly was exotic, but fairly innocuous. The can of Danish Ham was a different matter and came with what I think was caviar spread. Worse, the ham had an odd texture which I now know comes from the same process used to make lutefisk. If you don't know what that is, I'll not enlighten you. Look it up on the Web with a search for chemical compounds—chiefly lye.

There were five or six cans of various vegetables only somebody from the Balkans could identify or eat. I suspect they were used as penance for some inexplicable social sin that only Albanians recognize.

There were two cans of what was, according to the picture, the residue one gets from lingonberries if you mash them and spread them to dry on a wooden board for several days. I never could figure out why you'd want to get it to look like the picture on the can.

The real kicker, though, was the can I found of some French food. I actually ate some of that voluntarily, which goes to show what a rotten joker I was as a kid. I spotted an opportunity for an April Fools Day joke that ought to be in the Guinness Book of Records.

The alleged food turned out to be French Fried Silk Worms (hereafter called FFSW). After looking at the picture, I recognized a golden opportunity. They looked just like greasy corn curls. When April 1st rolled around about a week later, I cracked the can, dumped the contents of a bag of corn curls and substituted the FFSW. My sister observed sarcastically that it wouldn't work.

"They don't look that much like corn curls," she said.

I knew that. I'd already figured I'd have to lull my victim's suspicions and the only way I could do that would be if I volunteered to eat some myself.

I'm proud to say I didn't upchuck after eating four of them. I can still remember the taste and texture, but since this is a PG rated essay, I'll only describe the taste. They tasted so bloody bitter that they had no other taste whatsoever. On top of that, there was about a fifteen second delay on the taste, probably because the taste buds were stunned. In that fifteen second window I managed to talk six of my former best friends, two teachers and a poodle into trying them.

Once I told them what they'd actually eaten, the reaction was exciting. I never knew people gagged in so many different ways. I was lucky they didn't kill me.

Mechanically Sound

There's a common belief among Americans, particularly in the West and in rural areas, that every teenage boy is naturally interested in, drawn to, and in love with cars. It's harmless enough, I suppose, like most other misconceptions that don't kill you outright, but there are those who recognize their own limitations and have no interest in dwelling upon them.

You see, some people are really good at doing *some* things, but not others. I'm a whiz when it comes to taking things apart. There really aren't many things I can't disassemble, given some ordinary tools, WD-40, and a crowbar longer than eighteen inches. I can generally get things back together again, and have even gotten past that unsettling moment when one realizes that there are parts left over and no place to put them. The trick to that, by-the-way, is a large box labeled *Odds and Ends*.

The big problem is that they don't work after I'm done with them, which is no great loss. They weren't working when I started.

My first car was probably the best car I could have had, given that attitude. It was a 1963 Plymouth Valiant with what was called a slant six engine—I have no idea why. It seemed to sit upright in the front and I never once saw it tip one way or the other.

The slant six was a darn good engine, though, clearly designed by someone who had a good idea of the true abilities of teenage boys. Consequently, it was an engine awfully hard to kill, maim or humiliate. It even got great mileage sometimes, particularly downhill, and there was lots of open space around it in the engine compartment.

I think we paid something like $250 for it.

It got me where I needed to go ninety percent of the time, and the other ten percent, I probably didn't really need to be anyplace, anyway. I had great respect for that car. I never worked on it.

Still, there were a few things here and there that had to be adjusted or adjusted to. The three-speed gearshift on the column occasionally messed up and got locked in-between gears. That kind of threw me, the first couple of times it happened. It wasn't until a neighbor showed me what was wrong, that I adjusted to that quirk. There was a kind of rotary-collar thing-a-ma-jig that slipped on the column and one had to open the hood, wrestle with it a few minutes and then go on your way. As the car got older, it became more and more necessary to spray WD-40 around in the general vicinity as well.

The last half of my senior year, I had a different car (the Valiant docilely stayed in the driveway), made out of plastic, imitation wood grain, aluminum, and heavier plastic. It lasted for a good six months before it died. It was one of the first Subarus to hit the North American continent and while a polite car, it did seem to have something of a temper. At least, it didn't seem to like Oregon Coast rain all that much and let me know by having either the windshield wipers go out, or by leaking cold rainwater on my leg. How it was able to do that when it was 75 degrees out and not a cloud in the sky, remains a mystery to me.

My folks decided that it would be less expensive to get a different car when I went off to college, and we ended up getting a Ford Maverick—I felt comfortable with it because it had the gear shift back on the column where it was supposed to be and only three gears and reverse. And like a humble, but dear old friend, after the first 6000 miles, the gear shift loosened up and acted just like the Valiant's. Made me more comfortable, somehow.

Sometime late my freshman year the Maverick broke down and had to go to the shop for a week or two, and I needed something to drive back to the University of Oregon. Dad and I looked at the Valiant, started her up, and when it didn't sound like death warmed over, felt a great deal of relief. I could just take the Valiant to Eugene, big problem all solved.

Now at this point, I need to introduce you to one of my friends—a guy named Norman Gilmont. Norm was damn smart, and aching to get out of Toledo in a bad way, since he was stranded that weekend with no way to get back to Oregon State University. He gave me a call, knowing I had come back for the weekend and asked if I could drop him off on the way.

Norm, a wiry cuss, sporting dark eyes and hair complements of his partial Basque extraction, had no problem with riding in the Valiant, so I agreed to take him with me. He had, after all, ridden in it off and on for two years during high school. It turned out be a very good idea that he came along.

About half-way to Corvallis, we both heard a metallic snap and the engine went to idle. That bothered me a bit because I had had the pedal flat on the floor trying to keep my speed up as we finished the climb up Kline Mountain. We coasted to a stop on the top of the hill and parked. Norm said it didn't sound right.

I agreed. I'd driven that car for a couple of years and never heard it make noises like that one. With a certain reluctance we opened the hood and looked in.

Norm had me start the engine up again and then kick the gas pedal around while he watched for sparks, smoke, or signs of impending explosion. "Doesn't seem to work," he told me. I agreed. The pedal didn't feel like it was doing anything.

I got down on the floor and lifted up the pedal to discover that it was flapping free, and not connected to anything. I figured that might be the problem and told Norm, who nodded wisely, and said, "What's down there to attach the pedal to?"

I looked again and spotted a nubbin that didn't seem to want to go in or out. I tried twisting it and was rewarded with the sound of both a revving engine and one startled and very upset engine observer. Norm had been leaning over the engine and when it revved, the fan discarded a few chunks of dried mud. He poked his head in the open door and advised me that three seconds of warning were customary before trying to kill assistants.

He had a point.

We conferred. We tried to figure out how to attach the gas pedal, but had no success whatsoever. Whatever had done that duty before had disappeared, or at least gone into hiding. We bounced ideas off each other for five minutes before we discarded the usual unworkable solutions that people always get before accepting the inevitable.

I wracked my brain, all too aware that my mechanical abilities tended to be more dangerous than useful. But it suddenly occurred to me that quite a few things that metal linkages could do, a strong and desperate human hand might be able to do as well. I got Norm's attention away from the rain and explained my idea in a low, calm voice, the last being necessary due to the fact that out loud, my idea sounded daffy as hell.

"Maybe you could be the gas pedal," I said.

Norm's expression clearly indicated that my plan ranked right in there with getting smacked in the face with a sock full of quarters. I recognized it. His younger brother, Bob, had looked at me that way the time I'd been talked into climbing on top of the Toledo Swimming Pool, and dropping thirty feet into the not quite deep enough deep end.

As I've mentioned, however, Norm really wanted to get back to OSU, and hitching a ride in the rain from the summit of Kline Mountain couldn't be called an attractive alternative, particularly after the experience the two of us had had about four months before when the Maverick had run out of gas on our way to Toledo. I'd ended up hitching a ride into town, while Norm and one of his roommates had waved bye-bye from my car.

Norm wanted to know why he had to be the gas pedal. The Valiant was my car and would probably be offended if anybody else got so familiar with it.

I merely pointed out that I knew how to drive a manual transmission and he didn't, which more or less slammed the door on the discussion. With a certain amount of rueful grace, Norm positioned himself upside down on the passenger side and then contorted himself into position where he could grab the nubbin and twist.

Surprisingly enough it worked.

We finally limped into Corvallis about an hour later none the worse for our experience, though Norm was a trifle stiff. I always had the feeling after that, that Norm regarded riding with me in any car to be living dangerously, or at least uncomfortably. That was the only explanation I could come up with to account for the fact that he always carried a couple of crescent wrenches and half a roll of duct tape when I gave him rides in the future.

On the Road Again (or The Shopping Cart Blues)

I'd like to get Willie Nelson alone in a room with a can of cheese wiz, ten pounds of strawberries, and a cork core baseball bat for just five minutes...but I digress.

I had entertained the forlorn hope that I might finish out my stint with the Oregon Department of Transportation without being subjected to another move by management. It was a silly, childish dream I suppose, but an attractive one, nevertheless. Now, from the rumors that manage to find their way to me, I guess I should be thankful that I have a reasonable amount of lead time before my final ODOT journey begins. I can make things a bit easier on myself. I can begin to thin down the odds and ends I've accumulated over the last five years, and when the time comes, I'll be svelte enough from a possession point of view to once again take to shopping cart and trek the trackless wastes.

I'm the Traffic Section's designated wanderer.

No brag, just fact.

I'm not sure how that came about, but I suspect one of two things might be the cause. First, I might have been chosen because management figures I'm insanely adaptable and a good sport to boot. Or, second, I might have been picked because over the years, I've managed to win a special place in the heart of ODOT management. Perhaps a combination of the two.

Quite early in my career in the Marble Palace (as us Old Timers still call the ODOT building), I achieved a kind of Flying Dutchman mystique as a side effect of my prime directive—the reason I was hired for my job—programming. This was early in the computer revolution, and ODOT had only a few computers here and there, unless you count the terminals connected to the mainframe, and I don't. I hated mainframe programming because there always seemed to be a malicious element of chance involved. A program would run one time and then splat, refuse to compile or manufacture a closed loop that would run until the programmer's teeth fell out.

At that time, Traffic had a grand total of one and a half computers. That translated into one IBM PC and a Radio Shack TRaSh-80. I wasn't even stationed in the same room with either of them.

So, I took to wandering around the building like the Ghost of Christmas Future until I happened to find a PC that was currently unoccupied. I'd then slide into place very quietly, grab floppy disks, and program away, until the keeper of the PC came back and discovered my presence. Most of them took it pretty well, advising me that the PC wasn't assigned to me, and with cheerful kicks, slugs and verbal slights, eject me from my spot. One time in three, they'd write a nasty note to my supervisor.

Eventually, my programming requirements got the better of my meager resources, so I sat down, thought things out, and then bought my own laptop computer, which I proceeded to bring to work with me from that point on. I never regretted it and still bring my own computer to work.

My reputation for adaptability probably was forged at that time.

The last go-around came when it was decided that the top floor of the ODOT building needed to be remodeled along more conventional, modern, organizational lines. The problem was that we had offices and a hallway. We didn't have cubes.

That meant that we obviously couldn't communicate with each other—the walls being old fashioned ones, opaque and nearly sound proof. Plans were discussed, drawn up, discussed some more, a committee formed and then discussed. The new committee studied matters and talked about the floor plan, both the existing and the new, and then reported back, that yes, indeed, we were inefficient and needed something new to energize us. All of Traffic Section was thereupon renamed Traffic Management, and a study group put together to come up with a floor plan and reorganization. They met a couple of times, decided that the floor plan originally envisioned by management was spiffy, and the thing we should do.

They knocked out the east wall of my office a week later. Watching the wall go down, I decided I needed to move on with my life and then stopped, suddenly aware that that particular point had never been covered in any of the memos. I wasn't sure where I was supposed to settle down. I went to the office manager, Gerry.

"Where should I set up shop?" I asked.

Gerry looked puzzled. "Haven't you looked at the floor plan?"

I confessed that I hadn't, and with a big smile, Gerry led me to the Library/File room where the plan was sitting enshrined in one corner. He searched it for a moment and then pointed out my name. I looked at the spot and then looked around me. Unless I missed my guess, I was supposed to be put about twenty-five feet away, right where some signal design people were located. I said as much. Gerry nodded thoughtfully and fumbled around with the site map. He flipped a plastic transparency over the proposed map and then peered closely. Yep, I was ensconced right where Tom Jenkins currently sat.

I've known Tom Jenkins for over twenty years, and a more thoroughly likeable, affable soul would be hard to find. I can't recall a time where I've seen him really upset.

Even so, I kind of had the feeling that he might get a bit testy should I try to move in any time soon. I let Gerry know my concerns; once again he looked thoughtful for a moment and then allowed that I might have a point.

"So, where do you want me to go?"

You take the measure of a man, when you present him with such a dangerously open question; Gerry proved himself to be kind. He didn't tell me any of the first dozen or so places that I'm sure would have occurred to some people. Instead, he said words to the effect that he wasn't sure and that he'd get back to me. *Soon.*

Gerry went back to his office, and I went back to the remaining two walls of my old office. I think providence took a hand at this point because one of the office removers had taken the liberty of putting all of my stuff into a shopping cart that happened to be handy. I always wondered where it came from, but never was able to figure that out. The workmen all nodded at me agreeably, pointed me in the general direction of the remaining corridor, and went back to work.

Thus began my odyssey.

I spent the next six months living out of that shopping cart. I'd roll up to an open electrical outlet, plug in my computer AC adapter, lock down the wheels on both my shopping cart and chair and work. After a while, someone would come along and tell me that I was going to have to find someplace else, generally because more construction was underway but occasionally because they felt my tattered files and folders were unseemly. A couple of times I was simply told to *move along.*

I didn't get many phone calls during this period. That might show there's always a silver lining in any situation, or it could demonstrate simple-mindedness; I'm not altogether certain which.

One by one, the office walls came down and for a very, very brief time, I was not alone in my wandering. There were two others for a while at the beginning, but they didn't last. One guy took to hiding in the far northeastern corner, and after the third or fourth time he was ejected from his spot, he disappeared entirely. Rumor was that he had bribed somebody to get his position transferred to a different section. I don't know that that's the case, but there seems some truth, to it since he did reappear two or three weeks later on the staff list for the Project Analysis section in Planning. The other fellow wanderer of the fifth floor, being of a practical nature, simply checked his calendar and then checked out. That is, retired. He had over thirty years in, and went to live in Eastern Oregon as far away from any state highway as he could get whilst still remaining in Oregon.

Office cubes went up slowly and I took to stealing in after normal working hours and commandeering them. That would generally get me three or four days before I'd be ejected, my shopping cart again loaded, and put on the corridor. Onlookers might have been reminded of the waxing and waning of the tides.

Finally, most of the fifth floor had been converted to wall-less-ness and populated with cubes, all filled with happy campers working away. I kept my eye on the spot where I was supposed to eventually end up. It became apparent late that April, that my particular destination would be one of the last two places remodeled.

I felt like Moses standing on the edge of the Promised Land, forced to gaze from a distance and never to enter. Unlike Moses, however, I fully intended to ignore rules once the opportunity presented itself, and streak across the border and set up shop. I planned to become as difficult to remove as a barnacle, and when the second wall of my cube went up, I was there. Before you could say traffic operations, I was in place and not prepared to move for anybody or anything.

A problem cropped up, of course. The cube installers became agitated because they still had a few things to do—install shelves and lights for example, as well as the third wall. Gerry came down to talk to me, but paused a safe distance away when he saw my immediate reaction. I had grabbed a blowgun I had acquired in my wanderings, I forget where, that shot little suction cup tipped darts. I loaded it and stood at the ready. He politely pointed out from a safe distance that the cubicleers needed to finish my cube.

I don't recall my exact response, but I think I said something to the effect that they'd better be wearing Kevlar and toting body bags. Gerry nodded agreeably and went back to talk to the cubicleers.

They never did put up my third wall.

A well regulated office, being necessary to the security of a free cube, the right of the people to keep and bear blowguns, shall not be infringed.